Judy's Scary Little Christmas

Book by
David Church and Jim Webber

Music & Lyrics by
Joe Patrick Ward

A SAMUEL FRENCH ACTING EDITION

SAMUEL FRENCH

FOUNDED 1830

NEW YORK HOLLYWOOD LONDON TORONTO

SAMUELFRENCH.COM

ISBN 978-0-573-69805-7   Printed in U.S.A.   #29276

RENTAL MATERIALS

An orchestration consisting of a Piano/Vocal Score and Vocal Chorus Books will be loaned two months prior to the production ONLY on the receipt of the Licensing Fee quoted for all performances, the rental fee and a refundable deposit.

Please contact Samuel French for perusal of the musis materials as well as a performance license application.

IMPORTANT BILLING AND CREDIT REQUIREMENTS

All producers of *JUDY'S SCARY LITTLE CHRISTMAS* *must* give credit to the Author of the Play in all programs distributed in connection with performances of the Play, and in all instances in which the title of the Play appears for the purposes of advertising, publicizing or otherwise exploiting the Play and/or a production. The name of the Author *must* appear on a separate line on which no other name appears, immediately following the title and *must* appear in size of type not less than fifty percent of the size of the title type.

In addition the following credit *must* be given in all programs and publicity information distributed in association with this piece:

JUDY'S SCARY LITTLE CHRISTMAS
Book by
David Church and Jim Webber
Music and Lyrics by
Joe Patrick Ward

JUDY'S SCARY LITTLE CHRISTMAS was first produced by JSLC in association with The Victory Theatre in Burbank, California on November 17, 2002. The production was directed by Kay Cole, with musical direction by Joe Patrick Ward, sets by James Webber, costumes by Jeannine Campi, and Judy's gowns by Ricky Gilbert. The production stage manager was Jennifer Scheffer, and the production assistant was Sherri Taylor-Pilgren. The cast was as follows:

JUDY GARLAND	Connie Champagne
BING CROSBY	Sean Smith
LIBERACE	Don Lucas
ETHEL MERMAN	Lauri Johnson
RICHARD M. NIXON	Eric Anderson
LILLIAN HELLMAN	Jan Sheldrick
JOAN CRAWFORD	Joanne O'Brien
DEATH / VOICE OF DIRECTOR	Mark A. Cross
SAILOR	Dustin Strong
PUNCH (PUPPET)	Jim Hormel
ENSEMBLE	Charles Hererra, Heather Holland-Daly, Terri Homberg-Olsen, Jonathan Neely

CHARACTERS

JUDY GARLAND – The beloved show business icon of *The Wizard of Oz* and *A Star Is Born.* Judy is nervous and neurotic, but remains wildly talented and is fully primed for her biggest comeback ever.

BING CROSBY – The avuncular but alcoholic crooner of "White Christmas," whose greatest triumphs are behind him – and he knows it.

LIBERACE – The flamboyant Las Vegas pianist who brought highbrow music to lowbrow audiences. Lee is a smarmy mama's boy who masks the truth of his personal life with layers of camp.

ETHEL MERMAN – The bombastic Broadway star of *Annie Get Your Gun* and *Gypsy* whose belting voice and brassy manner accentuate her blunt ego.

RICHARD NIXON – A winner with flop sweat. The current Vice President is conniving, fearful, strangely sympathetic and completely out of place in this entertainment milieu.

LILLIAN HELLMAN – The chain-smoking playwright of *The Little Foxes* who was blacklisted as a Communist during the McCarthy era. Anger is both her tonic and her Achilles heel.

DEATH – All-knowing, immovable, forever. Death possesses the personality that every performer fears most – that of a truly discerning critic.

JOAN CRAWFORD – Hollywood's greatest self-made star who has gone from ingénue to leading lady to caricature and now is barricaded from reality as an ageless legend in her own mind

SAILOR – Handsome, clean-cut, observant, empathetic, gay – and not altogether who he appears to be.

DIRECTOR – An offstage voice. Focused and businesslike.

PUNCH – A goofy dragon hand-puppet.

ENSEMBLE – An attractive, effervescent quartet of two men and two women

Note: **SAILOR** and **DEATH** can double as **PUNCH** and the **DIRECTOR** (offstage voice)

SETTING

Studio A, CBS Television City, Hollywood.

TIME

Christmas Eve, 1959. Again.

AUTHORS' NOTES

Judy's Scary Little Christmas is a story about the holidays, ghosts and redemption. The premise ("Judy tries to stage her greatest comeback yet") is essentially dramatic but the plotline ("an oddball variety of stars re-create the past in a retro television special") is wholly comedic. All of it should be entertaining. To achieve this goal for your production, it's essential that your cast play the comedy for character as opposed to easy laughs. Yes, this is camp – but camp with brains. And heart.

Casting – While it's a bonus if your cast bears a dead-on physical resemblance to their respective celebrity roles, it's more important for your actors to approximate their vocal style and overall essence. The dialogue and lyrics have been specifically constructed to assist your actors in accomplishing this objective.

Tone & Pacing – It is important that the tone of the show walk the line between parody and nostalgic affection for the old TV Specials. Keep the pace of the book scenes steady. Don't let them get too frenetic in Act I or too slow in Act II. Also, use lighting changes to effectively differentiate the "on-camera" and "off-camera" sections.

Sets – The show takes us from a clear stage to Judy's "living room," then back to a clear stage and finally to a stylized "trolley" for the finale. All the set changes occur in view of the audience so any effects the designer and director can create to effect a smooth sense of flow will be of benefit. (We found that a traveler or curtain about ¾ of the way upstage offered enough clear space, provided a backing for the living room and masked the trolley upstage.) Judy's living room should epitomize television's idea of sumptuous living circa 1959. The finale's magical trolley can be either an ornate vehicle or as simple as a large cut out (with cut out windows) placed in front of a star curtain. If your trolley does not "move" then use a mirror ball and chaser lights to suggest the effect.

Please note: Certain song lyrics within the script are italicized. These denote lyrics that should be spoken within each musical number, not sung.

Special Thanks to Leonard Foglia, Eileen T'Kaye, Tim Choy,
Tom Astor, Brent Crayon, Allen Everman II, and Michael Lamont

(AT RISE: The set, seen in half-light, consists of an elegant front door upstage center.)

(The **DIRECTOR** *is heard from the booth via the P.A. system:)*

DIRECTOR. *(V.O.)* Thirty seconds to air. Camera one… camera two…camera three…check. Lights to black and…go.

(blackout)

In five – four – three –

(Lights up on the **HOLIDAY CHORUS;** *a choral quartet of two* **MEN** *and two* **WOMEN**. *They're dressed in colorful Dickensian apparel.)*

CHORUS.

GOD REST YE MERRY GENTLEMEN.
LET NOTHING YOU DISMAY.
REMEMBER CHRIST OUR SAVIOR
WAS BORN ON CHRISTMAS DAY.
TO SAVE US ALL FROM SATAN'S POWER
WHEN WE HAVE GONE ASTRAY.
OH, TIDINGS OF COMFORT AND JOY,
COMFORT AND JOY.
OH, TIDINGS OF COMFORT AND JOY.

(The tempo jumps to a jazzy finger-snapping bop.)

CHORUS.

JOY!
JOY, JOY, JOY!
JOY, JOY, JOY!

MM-BOP-A DOOBEDI-BOP!
SKOOP DE DOO!
BE-DOOBEDI-BOP!
WAH! SKA-DOO!

(They dance.)

CHORUS. *(cont.)*

OOOOH.
AAAH! AAAH!
AAAH! AAAH!
AAAH!!

(The doorbell chimes.)

DING, DONG!

(It chimes again.)

DING, DONG!
HERE IS THE STAR OF OUR SHOW!
AAAAAH.
AAAAAH!

*(The door opens and **JUDY GARLAND** appears. Applause. Contrary to those rumors you've heard, she looks sensational; in fighting trim and primed for her biggest comeback yet.)*

JUDY.

MY GOODNESS, I'M BACK HOME AGAIN.
I'VE MISSED YOU ALL SO MUCH.
I THANK YOU MERRY GENTLEMEN
FOR GREETING ME AS SUCH.

*(**JUDY** spots the studio audience.)*

JUDY.

I NOTICE THOUGH, THAT WE HAVE COMPANY.
SO LET'S ROCK-A-BYE OUR FRIENDS HERE
WITH A CHRISTMAS MELODY!
YOU SEE I'M…

BACK IN CHRISTMAS TOWN!
IT'S A HAPPY SORT OF HAVEN WHERE THE YULETIDE'S GAY.
BACK IN CHRISTMAS TOWN!
IT'S A MERRY LITTLE CHRISTMAS HERE EVERY DAY.

I'VE LONGED TO HEAR THOSE SLEIGH BELLS RING.
THEY REALLY MAKE MY HEARTSTRINGS ZING!
COME ON, LET'S SWING.
NO WOES TO GET US DOWN!

CHORUS.

DOO DOO DOO DOO DOO DOO DOO!

JUDY.

SO YELL…

JUDY & CHORUS.

"NOEL!"

JUDY.

I'M BACK IN CHRISTMAS TOWN!

JUDY.	**CHORUS.**
SOON THE JOINT'LL BE HOPPING –	OOOOOH.
YOU'LL BE GLAD YOU'RE HERE.	
WE'VE GOT FOLKS WHO WILL BE	OOOOOH.
DROPPING BY,	
THEY'RE ALL SO DEAR.	
WE'LL HAVE CAROLS AND A WHOPPING BIT	AAAHHH.
OF CHRISTMAS CHEER.	
SING…	

JUDY & CHORUS.

FA LA LA LA LA
LA LA LA LA LA!
BACK IN CHRISTMAS TOWN!

JUDY.

LIFE IS SUGAR PLUMS & "DECK THE HALLS" & MISTLETOE.

JUDY & CHORUS.

BACK IN CHRISTMAS TOWN!

JUDY.

YOU CAN LAUGH AWAY YOUR TROUBLES WITH A…

JUDY & CHORUS.

"HO HO HO!"

CHORUS.

HO HO
HO-DE-OH
HO HO HO HO!

CHORUS BOYS.

HEY, JUDY?

JUDY.

YES, BOYS?

CHORUS BOYS.

HEARD YOU HAPPEN TO LIKE NEW YORK.

JUDY.

OH, PHOOEY!

CHORUS GIRLS.

HOW ABOUT MEETING US IN ST. LOUIS?

JUDY.

GALS, THOSE CITIES MAY BE NICE,
BUT HERE'S ONE PLACE THAT'S PARADISE.
I'M…

JUDY & CHORUS.

BACK IN CHRISTMAS TOWN!

CHORUS BOYS.

SAY YOUR KENSINGTON AVENUE DAYS WEREN'T JOLLY?

JUDY.

HATED THE CLANG-CLANG OF THAT TROLLEY!

CHORUS GIRLS.

BUT SURELY YOU'LL MISS THE BOY NEXT DOOR?

JUDY.

GOT AN ELF NEXT DOOR NOW I LIKE MORE!

CHORUS.

AWWW!

JUDY & CHORUS.

BACK IN CHRISTMAS TOWN!
BACK IN CHRISTMAS TOWN!

CHORUS GIRL #2.

YOU'VE BEEN OVER THE RAINBOW!

JUDY.

YES, THAT'S TRUE.

CHORUS BOY #2.

BUT YOU LEFT THAT SCENE!

JUDY.

AND TOTO TOO.

CHORUS BOY #1.

BOUGHT A ONE-WAY TICKET...

CHORUS GIRL #1.

OUT OF OZ?

JUDY.

ON THE ATCHISON, TOPEKA
AND THE SANTA CLAUS!

(dance break)

CHORUS.

AH! WHOAH!
CLIP-CLOP! CLIP-CLOP!
GIDDY-UP, GO!

*(**JUDY** gestures to the **CHORUS**.)*

JUDY. Aren't they jolly?

CHORUS.

PEACE ON EARTH, GOOD WILL TO MEN!

JUDY. "The Merrymakers!"

CHORUS.

JUDY, WELCOME HOME.

JUDY. *(softly)*

THERE'S A FEELING WARM AND GLOWING
I FELT FROM THE START.
AND IT'S REALLY OVERFLOWING
DEEP WITHIN MY HEART.
WITH THE LOVE THAT YOU'RE ALL SHOWING,
HOW COULD I DEPART?
SING...

JUDY & CHORUS.

GLOOOOO...

JUDY.

...REEEAAAH!

(They wind up for the big finish.)

JUDY & CHORUS.
> BACK IN CHRISTMAS TOWN!
> HERE THERE'S NOTHING GRIM AT ALL,
> SO BABY, LOSE THAT FROWN!
> BACK IN CHRISTMAS TOWN!

JUDY.
> 'TIS THE SEASON ALL YEAR ROUN'!

CHORUS.
> *THE NIGHT'S NOT BITTER!*
> *THE STARS HAVE GOT THEIR GLITTER!*
> 'CAUSE LOOK WHO'S IN HER NEW LOCALE!

JUDY.
> HEY, ANDY HARDY,
> SO LONG, PAL!
> I'M BACK!
> I'M BACK!
> I'M BACK...
> BACK IN CHRISTMAS TOWN!!!

CHORUS.
> JUDY'S BACK IN CHRISTMAS TOWN!
> JUDY'S BACK IN CHRISTMAS TOWN!
> FA LA LA LA!

JUDY. *I'M BACK!*

> *(The applause sign cues the audience as it will through-out the show.)*

> *(Music. As* **JUDY &** *the* **CHORUS** *depart, lights change and the pieces of the Living Room Set are moved into place.)*

ANNOUNCER. *(V.O.)* From Television City in Hollywood, it's "Judy's Merry Little Christmas," starring Judy and her very special holiday guests.

> *(The fifties living room is more television special than actual home. Stage left is a a grouping of furniture that serves as the interview area. Stage right features a Christmas tree and a piano-bar that can be moved to create a performance space.)*

(Lights up full. Applause.)

JUDY. Hello, everybody. Welcome to my home. I can't tell you how delighted I am you're really here. The holidays are such a special time of year. At least they are for me. I'm sure they are for you, too. We're going to make this an evening of the best and the brightest. And that's what Christmas is all about, isn't it? Making spirits bright?
I've invited some marvelous guests. From Broadway, Hollywood, Las Vegas – even our nation's capital. Now, do we have everything? It seems I've forgotten something.

(She spins around and spots the Christmas tree.)

JUDY. Oh, my goodness.

(JUDY *flips the switch and the tree lights up.)*

JUDY. That's more like it, don't you think? Don't go away. We'll be right back.

(MUSIC)

DIRECTOR. *(V.O.)* We're clear.

(The lights change as they will during this and all subsequent commercial breaks.)

(JUDY *returns to downstage center and calls up to the booth:)*

JUDY. How was it, George?

DIRECTOR. *(V.O.)* It was great, Judy.

JUDY. Are you sure? You're not just, you know?

DIRECTOR. *(V.O.)* Ask the audience.

JUDY. Oh. Did you like the opening?

(The audience responds.)

JUDY. I'm so relieved because –

*(A burst of audio feedback is heard. **JUDY** looks at the booth.)*

God, what's that?

DIRECTOR. *(V.O.)* Sorry. We're fine.

JUDY. I hope so. I've got a lot riding on this one and it's got to be perfect. You got that?

DIRECTOR. *(V.O.)* Got it.

JUDY. Good.

*(A **DRESSER** enters with make-up and a hand mirror.)*

JUDY. Oh, dear I've got to...we can still talk.

DIRECTOR. *(V.O.)* Thirty seconds.

*(The **DRESSER** holds the mirror as **JUDY** checks her make-up.)*

JUDY. I haven't done a show like this in, I don't mind telling you, quite a while. I don't know what got into me exactly, it just seemed like it was time. But thank goodness, I've got all the best people –

(glancing at booth)

I think.

*(waving off the **DRESSER**)*

I don't know why I bother. Back at the studio, Lana Turner was always the glamorous one. They kept trying to make me into the girl next door. They couldn't even find the right house, let alone the right door.

*(The **DRESSER** offers **JUDY** a glass of wine. **JUDY** is tempted, but –)*

JUDY. No, thank you, dear.

*(The **DRESSER** exits.)*

JUDY. I think we'll have a wonderful time.

DIRECTOR. *(V.O.)* Ready in five, four, three...

(Music. applause.)

JUDY. Now you folks at home, sit back and, for goodness sake, relax. To a degree. After all, we're expecting company any minute.

(The doorbell chimes "Have Yourself A Merry Little Christmas.")

JUDY. That *must* be the doorbell.

(She opens the door, revealing...)

BING. Anybody seen a runaway golf ball?

JUDY. Bing Crosby!

(Applause. Music. **BING** *wears a corduroy hunting jacket and checkered hat, and carries his trademark golf club.)*

*(***BING** *hands* **JUDY** *his gold invitation, as will all her Guests.)*

BING. How's my little rainbow gal?

JUDY. Bing, why on earth are you...golfing on Christmas Eve?

BING. I thought I'd take a stroll on the links before the man with the reindeer comes in for a landing.

*(***JUDY** *laughs and takes* **BING**'*s golf club.)*

JUDY. You give me that, darling, and have a seat. Can I take your hat?

BING. Don't mind if you do. Give my brain doily a little oxygen.

JUDY. Bing, I can't tell you how good it is to see you.

BING. Look at you – you're as shiny as a snowflake.

*(***JUDY** *stores* **BING**'*s golf club in the fireplace tool stand.)*

JUDY. Why I haven't seen you since...well, since radio.

BING. We had some dandy times back then, didn't we, Judy?

JUDY. Oh, we did. I'm not much of a hostess. I haven't even offered you a refreshment.

BING. Now hold on. Before we make with the merry, I've got a little jingle-jangle just for you.

*(***BING** *gives her a jewelry box.)*

JUDY. My goodness...

*(***JUDY** *opens the box and takes out a yellowed parchment.)*

JUDY. It's an antique…piece of paper. And it's got some kind of writing on it. It looks like that Latin around the MGM Lion. Thank you, Bing. I can't read one word of this.

BING. Well, now, that's because it's all written down there in Gaelic.

JUDY. Gaelic?

BING. Yes, ma'am. What you're holding right there is none other than my Grandma Maggie's secret recipe for the Crosby Family Holiday Grog. What do you say I mix us up a batch?

JUDY. Of course, darling, it sounds delicious. But can you read Gaelic?

BING. I suppose I can make out a word or two. You know, there's a rumor going around that I'm Irish.

JUDY. Yes. And you know what they say about Irishmen?

(An Irish vamp is heard.)

BING. That sounds like my cue.

(Music continues as they go to the bar downstage right and don gay holiday aprons. The bar has been set-up as a makeshift kitchen complete with a giant simmering saucepan and a variety of "grog" ingredients.)

BING.
BACK IN LONGBEGONE TIMES IN THE DELLS OF KILLARNEY,
MY DEAR GRANDMA MAGGIE WOULD SMILE THE DAY
    THROUGH.
AND HER GLEE COULD BE FOUND
WHEN DECEMBER CAME 'ROUND
IN A HOLIDAY POTION SHE'D SECRETLY BREW.

JUDY. Bless her heart.

BING.
GRANDMA'S DRINK MADE FOLKS MERRY FROM DUBLIN TO
    DERRY.
TRADITION WOULD CARRY ON YEAR AFTER YEAR.
TO THIS DAY WE PREPARE IT.
WITH LOVED ONES WE SHARE IT…
A CUP OF HER FAMOUS AND FINE IRISH CHEER.

JUDY. Well, Bing, exactly how do you make this, uh, grog?

BING. Oh, it takes years of professional training. Watch out now! We've got some mighty potent spirits going into this concoction.

(Music switches to a swing beat as they make the grog.)

BING.

FIRST YOU FILL THE SAUCEPAN,
DADDY-O,
WITH THE HOT APPLE CIDER.
POUR IT IN AS SO.
BUH BUH BUH BUH BUH BUH BOO.
THE REST IS EASY, SWEETIE ONCE
YOU HAVE ALL YOUR INGREDIENTS.
YOU MIX 'EM WITH EXPEDIENCE.
YOU WITH ME, DARLIN'?

JUDY.

YES, SIR.

BING.

THEN COME HELP YOUR OL' PROFESSOR.
TO GIVE THE GROG A DANDY FIZZ,
A LITTLE PINCH OF GINGER IS
A REQUISITE.
BUT JUST A BIT!
ENOUGH TO GIVE A POW!
NOW NUTMEG IS ANOTHER SPICE
THAT GIVES A KICK.

JUDY.

MM, THAT SMELLS NICE.

BING.

LET'S DROP IT IN.

JUDY.

OKAY, SAY "WHEN."

BING.

ATTA GIRL,
WE'RE COOKIN' NOW!
IT'S A CHRISTMAS BEVERAGE.
RULE OF THUMB,
WE JUST GOTTA ADD A SUGARPLUM.

JUDY.

GUARANTEED TO CURE YOUR HUMBUG GLUM!

BING.

AIN'T IT TRUE?

JUDY.

YOU BET!

BING.

AND HOW!

(spoken) Hey, Judy, how about singing a chorus with me?

JUDY. That would be marvelous.

BOTH.

LET'S SHARE A CUP OF IRISH CHEER!

WE'LL TOAST THE SWELLEST TIME OF YEAR.

SING TA RA LOO,

IT'S CHRISTMAS, DEAR.

SO HERE'S TO ME AND YOU!

BING. Now back to the business at hand.

COCOA, YOU KNOW, HAS HUNDREDS OF USES.

CREAM, LET HER FLOW,

AND NEXT COME THE JUICES.

*(**BING** is distracted by an unseen figure blocking his cue cards offstage.)*

JUDY.

ORANGE JUICE!

BING.

LIME JUICE!

BOTH.

PUT 'EM IN THE POT!

BING.

GRAPE JUICE!

JUDY.

PRUNE JUICE!

BING. Prune juice? Mm, better not.

JUDY.

GEE, MAKING GROG CAN SURE BE FUN!

BING.

HEY, EASY ON THAT CINNAMON!

JUDY.

VANILLA, BING?

BING.

YOU DO YOUR THING!

MAN, YOU DON'T MISS A BEAT.

WISH GRANDMA MAGGIE WERE ALIVE.

JUDY.

HOW MANY CUPS OF SUGAR?

BING.

FIVE.

DON'T LOLLYGAG, JUST DUMP THE BAG!

THAT'S WHAT MAKES 'ER TASTE SO SWEET!

BOTH.

LET'S SHARE A CUP OF IRISH CHEER!

WE'LL TOAST THE SWELLEST TIME OF YEAR.

SING TA RA LOO,

IT'S CHRISTMAS, DEAR!

SO HERE'S TO ME AND YOU!

BING.

NOW HOLD YOUR HAT

AND LISTEN, YA'LL.

THE MOST IMPORTANT PART OF ALL.

THE KEY TO THE CROSBY FAMILY DRINK,

AND NO, IT'S NOT THE KITCHEN SINK.

(**BING** *produces a flask of whiskey.*)

BOTH.

AAAAAH!

BING.

SOME IRISH WHISKEY, IF YOU PLEASE.

OR SO THE RECIPE DECREES.

A SINGLE TEASPOON,

AND DON'T CHEAT…

(**BING** *carefully pours the whiskey into a teaspoon and adds a single drop to the final mix.*)

BING. *(cont.)*

...MAKES THE WHOLE DARN THING COMPLETE.

JUDY.

NEAT!

BOTH.

LET'S SHARE A CUP OF IRISH CHEER!
WE'LL TOAST THE SWELLEST TIME OF YEAR.
SING TA RA LOO,
IT'S CHRISTMAS, DEAR.
SO HERE'S TO ME AND YOU!

*(***BING*** ladles the grog into two mugs for* **JUDY** *and himself.)*

JUDY. And to everybody watching!

BOTH.

YES, HERE'S...
HERE'S TO ME AND YOU!

BING. Down the chimney.

*(***JUDY*** and* **BING** *clink their mugs together and drink. Applause.)*

DIRECTOR. *(V.O.)* And...we're clear.

*(***JUDY*** and* **BING** *spit out the grog and grimace.)*

JUDY. It's like drinking a wedding cake.

BING. Grandma Maggie had quite the sweet tooth.

JUDY. I'm surprised she had any teeth at all.

(The **DRESSER** *clears the grog items.* **BING** *produces two liquor bottles.)*

JUDY. But darling, you were wonderful. The way you juggled all those bottles and everything.

BING. Just my recipe in swingtime. But I had a little problem there seeing those idiot cards.

JUDY. Really? I didn't notice.

BING. Some big, tall fellow blocking my view.

(A mysterious musical chord. **JUDY** *looks up in panic.)*

JUDY. Oh. Dear.

(**JUDY** *grabs the vodka bottle.*)

(nervously) Give me that. You just watch now and I'll show you how to make Grandma *Garland's* Holiday Grog.

(**JUDY** *pours the vodka into two new mugs.*)

BING. Say, is this a complicated recipe?

JUDY. It's a snap. One step.

(They clink and drink.)

BING. Grandma Garland sure knows how to put the fifth in the twenty-fifth.

JUDY. That's the idea.

DIRECTOR. *(V.O.)* Thirty seconds.

JUDY. Let's sit over here, darling.

(They return to the couch with their mugs as the piano-bar is re-positioned Downstage Right and a candelabra is set.)

JUDY. Now tell me, how's the family? How's...Karen?

BING. Kathryn. She's a –

JUDY. – Kathryn –

BING. – fine little gal. She's given me a whole new lease on life. "Second Time Around."

JUDY. And how are your boys? Gary and Lindsey and the twins?

BING. Your guess is as good as mine. No time for the old man anymore. Unless they're broke or in jail.

DIRECTOR. *(V.O.)* Fifteen seconds.

JUDY. *(changing the subject)* You know, I used to do all this by myself – the hard way. Not anymore.

(taking his hand)

I'm glad you found time for me.

DIRECTOR. *(V.O.)* In five...four...

JUDY. *(re: mugs)* Should we keep the props?

DIRECTOR. *(V.O.)* Sure, why not? Three...

JUDY. Oh, good.

(*Lights. Music.* JUDY *and* BING *erupt into phony stage laughter.*)

JUDY. I think we're back. Bing, do you have a favorite holiday tradition? Besides, the uh, grog?

BING. Yes, ma'am. Every Christmas Eve, the Crosby Quintet goes out a-caroling.

JUDY. (*uncertain*) Oh…you and your boys?

BING. Gary and Lindsey and the tintinnabulatin' twins. Sometimes they even let the old man sing one of his favorite numbers – about a particular Christmas…

(*singing*)

"…where the tree tops glisten and children listen…

JUDY. (*knowingly to audience*) That's everyone's favorite.

BING. "…to hear sleigh bells in the snow."

(*Applause. The doorbell rings, chiming* Have Yourself A Merry Little Christmas.)

BING. Upstaged again.

JUDY. That's one of *my* favorite numbers. Excuse me.

(JUDY *opens the door.*)

JUDY. Liberace!

(*APPLAUSE. Music.* LIBERACE *enters, resplendent in a velvet dinner jacket with piano key lapels and a knitted scarf with bells. He carries an ornately wrapped gift.*)

LIBERACE. "Judy, Judy, Judy." And that, ladies and gentlemen, concludes my entire performance as Mr. Cary Grant.

JUDY. Oh, Lee. Here, let me take your beautiful scarf.

LIBERACE. Thank you, Judy. And thanks for the invitation.

(*He hands* JUDY *his invitation.*)

LIBERACE. You know, I just love your chimes.

JUDY. (*jingling his scarf*) I love yours, too. You know Bing Crosby.

LIBERACE. I certainly do. Put her there, Bing.

(As **JUDY** *hangs up his scarf,* **LIBERACE.** *extends a limp, bejeweled hand to* **BING.** *who grudgingly shakes it.)*

BING. Whoa-ho, it's the music man himself.

JUDY. You two boys have a seat. Lee, would you care for some of Bing's holiday grog? It's an old family recipe.

LIBERACE. Mm, that sounds festive. You know, speaking of recipes, the Liberace family likes to whip up some delicious holiday treats of their own. In fact, Mother sent this batch over with her best wishes.

(He hands the box to **JUDY.** *)*

JUDY. Oh, Lee, that's so...

(She removes the lid.)

JUDY. Sweet rolls?

LIBERACE. "Liberace's Sticky Buns."

*(***JUDY** *displays the buns.)*

JUDY. They're still warm! Did you make these all by yourself?

LIBERACE. Actually, Mother does the baking in her very own oven but she lets me squirt on the glaze.

*(***JUDY** *quickly covers the box.)*

JUDY. Bing and I were talking about our favorite Christmas traditions. I'm sure you have one, too.

LIBERACE. As a matter of fact, I do. Once a year on Christmas Eve, mother and I drive down to the Long Beach Naval Station and invite a lonely serviceman home to share a piping hot dinner with all the trimmings. And Judy, have I got a surprise for you.

JUDY. Really?

LIBERACE. That young serviceman is backstage tonight.

JUDY. He is? He's here? Well, let's bring him out, shall we?

LIBERACE. Ladies and gentlemen, Seaman Timothy Russell!

("Anchors Aweigh" cues applause as the **SAILOR,** *a military stud, enters and salutes the audience.)*

JUDY. May I call you Tim? And you can call me Judy.

SAILOR. Yes, ma'am.

JUDY. Where are you from, Tim?

SAILOR. Lawton, Oklahoma. I never thought I'd get to be on TV.

JUDY. Is there anyone back home you'd like to say hello to?

SAILOR. My Mom and Dad, kid sister, Donna, friends. Merry Christmas everybody. God bless us every one.

JUDY. Isn't that lovely? Seaman Timothy Russell.

("Anchors Aweigh" plays again. **JUDY** *starts the applause and pulls him in for a kiss on the cheek. He shyly obliges, salutes the audience and leaves.)*

JUDY. I think Christmas really *is* the season of giving.

LIBERACE. You sure said a mouthful. Give till it hurts. Even if you have to –

JUDY. Lee, I'm sure you have some other, *family* traditions.

LIBERACE. I certainly do. In our home, this wondrous time of year wouldn't be complete without the gift of music. In fact, Judy, I feel like doing a little gift-giving right now.

JUDY. Please, be my guest.

(She leads the audience in applause as **LIBERACE** *moves to the piano-bar. The candelabra lights up as the lights in the interview area go out and* **JUDY** *and* **BING** *go off-stage.)*

LIBERACE. There are so many wonderful old traditional carols, but tonight, I'd like to start a new tradition. The young people today have a hep new sound all their own. I call this one, "The Candy Cane Twist." I hope you dig it.

*(***LIBERACE** *launches into a boogie-woogie number which builds to a musical "break." The first time this happens, an* **AUDIENCE MEMBER** *shouts out:)*

AUDIENCE MEMBER. YEAH!

LIBERACE. *(vamping underneath)* You know, it's funny. Whenever I come to that break, someone always seems to go wild. The rhythm just brings out the beatnik in 'em.

So this time, if you feel like shouting "Yeah," go right ahead.

(Music resumes. At the break the **AUDIENCE** *shouts:)*

AUDIENCE. YEAH!

(He turns slyly to the audience.)

LIBERACE. You wanna do it again, don'cha?

(Music resumes.)

AUDIENCE. YEAH!

(One candelabra bulb goes out. **LIBERACE** *reacts. This recurs with each "Yeah.")*

LIBERACE. This time, just the ladies.

LADIES. YEAH!

LIBERACE. Okay, fellas, now it's your turn.

FELLAS. YEAH!

LIBERACE. Oh, come on guys, you can do better than that.

FELLAS. YEAH!!!

LIBERACE. And they say I only excite the women. Okay, everybody, one last time!

(He returns to the main theme and builds to the break.)

ALL. YEAH!

(The last bulb goes out as **LIBERACE** *ends the song in grand concerto style. As he acknowledges the applause, the five lights eerily return to full brightness. When he turns to see them, they dim out.)*

*(***JUDY** *and* **BING** *come back onstage.)*

JUDY. Darling, that was smashing.

BING. Say, Daddy-O, that's one way-out work-out.

LIBERACE. *(still rattled)* I'm delighted you both enjoyed it.

(A familiar, foghorn voice sings a capella offstage: **ETHEL MERMAN**.*)*

ETHEL. *(off)*
...ROUND YON VIRGIN, MOTHER AND CHILD...

JUDY. I certainly know who that is.

ETHEL. *(off)*

...HOLY INFANT, SO TENDER AND MILD...

LIBERACE. Here come those chimes.

(Instead of ringing the doorbell, ETHEL knocks loudly on the door.)

ETHEL. *(off)*

...SLEEP IN HEAVENLY PEACE...

(JUDY opens the door, revealing ETHEL MERMAN. Her ensemble: a flowered print dress, straw hat, large rattan handbag, chunky jewelry, and a Hawaiian lei slung around her neck.)

(ETHEL plants herself centerstage and finishes the song.)

ETHEL.

...SLEEP IN HEAVENLY PEACE!

JUDY. Ethel Merman!

(Applause. Music. ETHEL bows to the audience and turns to JUDY.)

ETHEL. Hiya, Judy...Bing...Maestro.

ALL. Hello, Ethel, etc.

ETHEL. I see you bums started the party without me. Guess I've got some catching up to do.

JUDY. Darling, it's never a party until you show up.

ETHEL. Thanks, kid.

JUDY. Bing, would you get Ethel some grog? Please everybody, let's sit down.

(They enter the living room.)

JUDY. Ethel, my word, you look wonderful.

ETHEL. What can I tell you, I'm in a holiday mood.

JUDY. Yes, but what holiday? You look like you're ready for the "Easter Parade."

ETHEL. Is that so? You know what they say: Christmas in Tinseltown – "Anything Goes."

(ETHEL takes her drink from BING.)

ETHEL. Thanks, Bingo.

(takes a sip, shudders, and smiles)

Say, that really hits the spot.

JUDY. Speaking of hits, darling, I hear you're wonderful in "Gypsy."

(applause)

ETHEL. Oh, yeah? Thanks. I keep busy.

JUDY. And how's your old chum, Mary Martin? She's supposed to be *sensational* in "The Sound of Music."

ETHEL. You don't say? Haven't seen it. She keeps sending me comps. Funny. I'm a smash in a show about a stripper and all of a sudden she opens down the street playing a nun.

JUDY. That *is* a coincidence.

ETHEL. You think so? Anyway, I finally got a vacation and I just flew in from Honolulu. Six and a half hours of loop the loop. Thank God I had some peanut brittle to settle my stomach. At any rate, I booked myself into Waikiki for some tropical R&R. You ever been?

(before they can respond)

Yeah, well, no sooner did I set foot in the celebrity suite at the Royal Hawaiian, than I was zipped off to a real-live, honest-to-Pete luau. And do they ever lay out a smorgasbord.

JUDY. Don't they have those hula girls?

ETHEL. Are you kidding? They've got hula girls, they've got fire dancers, they've even got a bunch of fellas strumming ukuleles in their BVD's.

LIBERACE. You don't say?

ETHEL. And the music, oh, Judy, the music! When I heard that native beat, I said to myself, "Ethel Agnes, this thing's a gold mine – start digging." So I got on the horn to Billy May, he whipped up some charts, and I put the whole shebang down on wax. Which reminds me, Merry Christmas.

(**ETHEL** *yanks out a record album from her handbag and plugs it.*)

JUDY. Oh, look everybody – it's called "Ethel Goes Hawaiian. Traditional Island Melodies With A Broadway Beat."

ETHEL. We made a couple of changes…for America.

JUDY. Ethel, I'm sorry, my hi-fi's on the blink. Could you sing something for us?

ETHEL. I guess I'll have to! That is if "fingers" here'll back me up on the old pianola.

LIBERACE. It would be my pleasure, Miss Merman.

(**JUDY** *leads the audience in applause as* **LIBERACE** *returns to the piano and begins vamping.* **JUDY** *and* **BING** *exit.*)

ETHEL. Now what we've got here is an ancient lullaby about a beautiful island girl who's in love with a handsome island boy. You know, they say that falling in love is wonderful – and I oughta know! But these kids can't make it legal because she ain't even got two puka shells to string together and his Pop's the King of the Great Manitupi. The poor slob's a Prince. Get it? Hit it!
THERE'S A NATIVE TUNE
SUNG BENEATH THE ISLAND MOON
THAT RECALLS THE STORY OF
A BOY AND GIRL WHO FALL IN LOVE.

"FOREVER YOURS" THEY SWORE
ON THEIR DREAMY TROPIC SHORE.
IN EACH OTHER'S ARMS THEY FELT AS FREE
AS BROKEN DRIFTWOOD DRIFTING OUT TO SEA.

(*The* **CHORUS** *enters. The* **GIRLS** *wear grass skirts. The* **BOYS** *strum Ukuleles.*)

ETHEL & CHORUS.
MAUNA LOA HULA HOLIDAY.
THAT WAS THE LOVELY DAY YOU CAME MY WAY.
I'LL KISS YOU WHILE THE PALM TREES GENTLY SWAY.
AND HERE WITHIN MY HEART YOU'LL ALWAYS STAY.

ETHEL. Now just when our two lovebirds are all set to elope, the King gets wise and cuts in on the act.

YES, THE BOY'S OLD MAN

CONJURES UP THIS AWFUL PLAN...

"I SHALL GRANT THE MARRIAGE, YES I SHALL,

IF SHE PROVES HERSELF A WORTHY GAL."

You get what I'm saying?

HE HAD A SCHEME!

A HORRIBLE SCHEME!

CHORUS.

LOOK UP THERE!

ETHEL.

IT'S MAUNA LOA!

CHORUS.

VOLCANO FAIR!

ETHEL.

LIKE KRAKATOA!

And Poppa King lays it right on the line.

"TELL THE GIRL SHE'LL FEEL NO PAIN, NO!

JUST ONE THING THAT I REQUIRE.

THROW HERSELF IN THE VOLCANO

TO APPEASE THE GOD OF FIRE.

THEN WE'LL PULL HER OUT, AND IF SHE ISN'T DEAD,

SHE'S THE BROAD OUR MIGHTY GOD WANTS YOU TO WED!"

And when those drums start beating, Little Princie almost has a heart attack.

CHORUS.

MALI ONA PU-E-HO

LELI KAHI WIKI PA!

ETHEL. Which means "It's a Lovely Day For Roasting Virgins."

CHORUS.

MALI ONA PU-E-HO

LELI KAHI WIKI PA!

ETHEL. By this time, Sweet Leilani's all dolled up for the shake 'n bake and, with the whole village watching, they shove her out onstage.

CHORUS.
> KE-A-LO-HA
> WIKI WIKI MAI TAI!

ETHEL. Here she is, Boys!

CHORUS.
> NEI-NO E DELIGHTFUL!
> WAI-KU I DELOVELY!

ETHEL. And the little lady's screaming bloody murder... "I Won't Go!"

CHORUS.
> YES, YOU WILL!

ETHEL.
> "NO, I WON'T!"

CHORUS.
> YES, YOU WILL!

ETHEL.
> "NO, I WON'T!"

CHORUS.
> YES, YOU WILL!

ETHEL.
> "NO, I WON'T!"
> "NO, I WON'T!!"

CHORUS.
> HIKI-LA-HA PUI HONE
> EK-ROL MIS-TA GOLD-STONE!

ETHEL. And the natives are drumming and chanting and doing what comes naturally – they're trying to wake up the great God Mauna Loa by dancing their ritual fire dance.

CHORUS.
> WIK-WIKI MAUNA LOA BLOW!
> WIK-WIKI MAUNA LOA BLOW!

ETHEL.

BLOW MAUNA LOA BLOW!

I SAY BLOWWW!

CHORUS.

WIK-WIKI MAUNA LOA BLOW!

(repeat seven times)

ETHEL.

BLOWWW!!

(THUNDER! The lights flicker and go out. When they come up, the **BOYS** *are shirtless and wearing grass skirts, while the Hula* **GIRLS** *sport Hawaiian trunks.)*

*(***ETHEL** *is visibly thrown by this, but continues with the number.)*

ETHEL.

THE LAVA SHOT OUT.

THE GOD WAS STEAMED.

THE GIRL WAS DOOMED.

BUT THE PRINCE, HE SCREAMED,

"ENOUGH, POPPA!

YOU'RE TOUGH, POPPA!

BUT I'M THROUGH SHAKING

AND TAKING THIS BULL FROM YOU...

SO I'M JUMPING IN, TOO!"

CHORUS.

OOOH. OOOH.

OOOH. OOOH.

ETHEL. Course when the King hears this, he says, "Let's call the whole thing off" – and he don't mean the wedding. Before you can say "Pineapple Princess," the two kids clinch the deal, Poppa declares a big holiday and they all sit down to dinner. Everything is wonderful, wonderful.

ETHEL & CHORUS.

MAUNA LOA HULA HOLIDAY.

THAT WAS THE LOVELY DAY YOU CAME MY WAY.

I'LL KISS YOU WHILE THE PALM TREES GENTLY SWAY.

AND HERE WITHIN MY HEART YOU'LL ALWAYS STAY.

ETHEL.
> AND EVERY DAY, I'M GLAD TO SAY,
> IS A HULA HOLIDAY
> WITH YOU!
>
> *(Applause.* **JUDY** *crosses to* **ETHEL** *and gestures. Music.)*

JUDY. Ethel Merman, everybody! Don't go away.

DIRECTOR. *(V.O.)* ...and, we're clear!

> *(***ETHEL** *drops her smile and turns angrily on* **JUDY.***)*

ETHEL. Jesus Christ, Judy, what kind of nickel and dime joint are you running here? Can't you pay your light bill?

JUDY. I thought that was part of your act.

ETHEL. And what's up with you dames?

CHORUS BOYS. We're sorry, Miss Merman. We don't know what happened.

ETHEL. That makes three of us. And who's this crazy spook on the loose?

JUDY. What? Where?

ETHEL. You name it. Backstage, out front, in the wings.

LIBERACE. I think I saw him, too.

JUDY. You did?

> *(***BING** *and the* **CHORUS BOYS** *agree.)*

BING. A shadowy kind of fella.

JUDY. *(into the wings:)* Did anyone else...you did!

> *(to booth:)*

> George! Everyone says there's someone down here running around. It's making us very nervous.

DIRECTOR. *(V.O.)* I'll get security right on it.

JUDY. You do that. Because, I mean, for heaven sakes –

ETHEL. *(suddenly remembering)* Hold the phone, Georgie! I know who it is. Red Skelton's taping a Christmas Carol sketch down the hall and this guy's playing some kinda ghost. He just popped across the hall to hear me belt one out of the park.

JUDY. I should've thought of that.

BING. Are you sure?

ETHEL. Sure I'm sure. Everybody loves the Merm.

(to Hula Boys)

Scram!

JUDY. *(covering)* That's got to be it. Drinks, anyone?

LIBERACE. More grog?

ETHEL. Not that candy-ass cider – I want a *drink.*

BING. *(checking the bar)* I'm afraid, Mother Hubbard, the cupboard is bare.

JUDY. Not necessarily.

*(**JUDY** gestures and the Christmas tree revolves, revealing a well-stocked Liquor Cabinet.)*

BING. Whoa, Tannenbaum!

JUDY. I hate to run dry during the holidays.

*(They converge on the bar. **BING** seizes a bottle of Irish whiskey.)*

BING. I must've been a good boy, after all. Old Santa even knows my favorite brand.

*(**BING** retreats to the far side of the set where he drinks alone.)*

LIBERACE. *(stepping behind bar)* Ladies, allow me.

JUDY. How sweet.

LIBERACE. Shall I "Make It Another Old-Fashioned," Miss Merman?

ETHEL. Very funny. Vodka rocks, straight up.

JUDY. Uh...ditto.

*(As **LIBERACE** pours the drinks:)*

JUDY. Your children must have adored Hawaii.

ETHEL. Hmphf! They practically went native on me. We got Bob one of those crazy surfboards and we signed Ethel, Jr. up for hula lessons. Get a load of this.

*(She shows **JUDY** a snapshot.)*

ETHEL. *(cont.)* Little grass skirt, coconut bra…look at her selling it.

JUDY. Like mother, like daughter.

ETHEL. "Little Miss Broadway," that's what we call her.

(a beat)

Goddamn cute.

(re: her drink)

What the hell's this?

LIBERACE. Vodka?

JUDY. Oh, no, no.

ETHEL. That's just enough to piss me off. Put some balls on it, twinkletoes.

(LIBERACE *pours.)*

ETHEL. Keep going. Keep going. Jackpot.

(to **JUDY***)*

Your kids?

JUDY. They're marvelous. They're growing like weeds, all three of them. I really wish you could see them. They're, uh…with Sid.

(LIBERACE *pours a neat crème de menthe and crosses to* **BING.***)*

LIBERACE. *(re:* **BING***'s jacket)* Say, Bing, that's a sporty number you've got on there.

(BING *ignores him. A pause.)*

LIBERACE. I'm just wild about corduroy.

BING. *(irritated)* Hey pal, I'm drinking here, will ya?

LIBERACE. *(stung)* Oh. Sure.

(LIBERACE *stands awkwardly for a moment. Judy sees this. He turns to the audience.)*

LIBERACE. Hiya, folks, are you enjoying the show? Wonderful. Would you like to see my rings? The diamond figure eight? That was a gift from my dear friend, Sonia Henie. When it comes to picking the ice, Sonia's an expert.

DIRECTOR. *(V.O.)* Sixty seconds.

(**JUDY** *goes downstage to* **LIBERACE.** **ETHEL** *follows.*)

JUDY. Lee, what's going on down there?

LIBERACE. I'm having an intimate conversation with some new friends.

JUDY. I hope you're not telling any dirty stories.

ETHEL. *(to* **JUDY***)* Yeah, what's that one you were telling me backstage…about Milton Berle?

JUDY. Oh, uh – that's not exactly a Christmas story.

ETHEL. *(indicating the audience)* You think they give a rat's ass? Tell it!

JUDY. *(giving in)* Milton Berle and Forrest Tucker were in the locker room at the Hillcrest Country Club and for years everyone said they had the two biggest… thing-a-ma-bobs in show business. Well, Jackie Gleason decided to have a contest, so all the members bet a thousand dollars to see which one, Milton or Forrest, had the biggest…

ETHEL. Schlong.

JUDY. Yeah. Now Forrest had no problem exposing his…

JUDY & ETHEL. Schlong –

JUDY. – to anyone. But Milton absolutely refused. So Jackie said, "Nobody's asking you to show the whole thing, Milton – just take out enough to win."

(They all laugh riotously.)

DIRECTOR. *(V.O.)* Fifteen seconds…

JUDY. That's quite enough of that. Shall we?

(She leads them back to the living room set as the Christmas tree revolves to hide the liquor.)

LIBERACE. Should we hide our drinks?

JUDY. Oh, well, uh…

ETHEL. Click those red shoes together. Make 'em disappear.

JUDY. Don't you make fun of my ruby slippers. I've come a long way in those shoes –

ETHEL. – You're telling me –

JUDY. – And they've saved my ass. More than once.

DIRECTOR. *(V.O.)* In five – four – three…

JUDY. Did someone fart?

(Laughter. Music. Applause. Doorbell.)

JUDY. You know, every time that rings I've got to pay Metro a royalty.

(She opens the door to reveal…)

JUDY. Richard Nixon!

(Applause. Music. NIXON flashes a constipated smile and steals a furtive glance into the wings. He is clearly out of his league in this show business milieu.)

NIXON. Good evening, Judy – and everyone. I just happened to be in the neighborhood doing some last minute shopping.

JUDY. I can't tell you how honored I am. It's not everyday I have a real live vice-president in my very own living room.

NIXON. Just look at you, Judy. You're all grown up. But you know, I'll always think of you as that little girl who dreamed of going over the rainbow.

JUDY. Oh, yes. I think you know Ethel Merman.

ETHEL. Hiya, Veep!

NIXON. I had the pleasure of meeting Miss Merman at the GOP Convention.

JUDY. And I'm sure you've heard of Bing Crosby.

NIXON. Pat and I have enjoyed your fine performances in radio, television and motion pictures.

BING. Well, I'm much obliged.

JUDY. And this is Liberace.

NIXON. Oh, yes, the young man with the candelabra. I want to thank you for bringing the classics into the homes of all Americans. Even the Democrats.

LIBERACE. Thank you, Mr. Vice President.

NIXON. And now…farewell.

JUDY. Leaving so soon? I wouldn't hear of it. My little party's just beginning.

(JUDY rattles her head. She's heard that line somewhere before.)

NIXON. No, no. I just stopped by to say season's greetings, happy holidays and Merry Christmas.

JUDY. Please give your family our best wishes. Richard Nixon, everybody!

(JUDY leads the applause. Playoff music. However, NIXON doesn't leave.)

NIXON. You, uh, seem to be having quite a celebration.

JUDY. *(puzzled)* Yes. It's a shame you have to go.

NIXON. Yes, indeed. "I'll be home for Chirstmas."

(Playoff music again. NIXON still doesn't leave. Judy shoots a worried look to the booth.)

NIXON. Quite a celebration.

JUDY. You're going to miss quite a celebration if you don't hurry home to your family. Now.

NIXON. The truth is Pat and the girls are back in Washington. I'm afraid I'm...alone.

JUDY. On Christmas Eve? Well, I...I can't have that. You march right in and join the party. Bing, get him a drink.

BING. Sure thing. What's your poison?

NIXON. Since it's Christmas, how about a hot chocolate? And don't be stingy with the marshmallows.

(NIXON laughs. BING shudders and gets the cocoa. An uncomfortable silence.)

JUDY. So how's everything in...uh, Washington?

NIXON. Never better. Except for the Communist threat that eats away at the very heart of our American way of life.

(more uncomfortable silence)

BING. Here's your cocoa.

NIXON. Thanks, Bing.

(**NIXON** *slowly sips his cocoa.*)

JUDY. You hungry? We've got some rolls.

LIBERACE. Sticky buns.

NIXON. Why, thank you. You know, Julie and Tricia are as busy as bees in the kitchen this time of year. Plum puddings, petit fours, fruit cakes.

NIXON. *(re: the sticky bun)* Delicious!

JUDY. They say that men actually make the best chefs. Are you…?

NIXON. No, no…I am not a cook.

(The show grinds to a halt as **NIXON** *meticulously finishes the sticky bun and cleans his fingers.)*

*(***JUDY*** *launches into a segue.)*

JUDY. That reminds me, a number of years ago, I made a picture called "Meet Me In St. Louis."

(applause)

JUDY. Thank you.

(Piano under. Lights dim. **JUDY** *walks into a spotlight.)*

JUDY. And I remember, whenever I'd go on the set, it was like walking back into another time. I loved making that picture and I've often thought, wouldn't it be marvelous if we could jump onto a magical trolley and journey back to our favorite Christmases of yesteryear?

*(***JUDY*** *prepares to sing. From the dark,* **NIXON** *interrupts:)*

NIXON. I certainly remember *my* favorite Christmas.

JUDY. *(pointedly)* So do I.

(singing:)

WITH MY HIGH-STARCHED COLLAR
AND MY HIGH-TOPPED SHOES
AND MY HAIR –

NIXON. The year was 1925 and father was in a deep depression.

(The music peters out. **NIXON** *continues, oblivious.)*

NIXON. To cheer him up, I started to sing a popular song of the day entitled "I Want To Be Happy."

(JUDY gives up and heads to the piano bar for a drink.)

NIXON. For some reason, my attempt at merrymaking drove father into an inexplicable rage and he proceeded to beat the living daylights out of me.

(The others shift uncomfortably.)

NIXON. What was it that triggered father's turbulent moods? Was it the bitter failure of the lemon ranch? Who can say? Later that night, I asked my sainted mother, Hannah, "Why did father beat me so? Why were we poor? Why were there no presents under the tree. Why was there no tree?"

*(As **NIXON** pauses to clear his throat, it's clear that everyone is appalled by his story.)*

NIXON. "It's true," admitted mother, "I have no store-bought present for you. But I have a gift of greater meaning." And with that, she took a rusty nail, attached it to an old piece of twine and tied it around my neck. "Son, let this nail represent the greatest gift that anyone has ever given mankind. The sacrifice of Christ's blood on the cross for your sins." And you know, Judy, it was the best Christmas present I ever got.

JUDY. *(stunned)* We'll be right back.

(Music. Lights change.)

DIRECTOR. *(V.O.)* We're clear. Two minutes.

JUDY. What the hell is wrong with you?

NIXON. I beg your pardon?

JUDY. You've got the timing of a subpoena.

NIXON. I don't understand.

JUDY. You completely blew the intro to my trolley number.

NIXON. We were talking about Christmas memories and –

JUDY. Look, bub, when the lights go down on you and the spot comes up on me, that's my cue to sing and your cue to SHUT UP!

NIXON. If you wanted some high-society pretty boy, why didn't you invite Jack Kennedy?

JUDY. I tried. Unavailable. Jesus! Ethel, you voted for him, you tell him.

(to booth:)

George, how much are we over?

ETHEL. Look, Dick, you've got to give the people what they want. It's Christmas Eve and you're crucifying 'em!

DIRECTOR. *(V.O.)* Two and a half.

JUDY. How long's the trolley number?

BING. And I'd cut that part about whipping the nipper. I used to beat my boys till their butts turned bloody but that's not the sort of thing you want to publicize.

DIRECTOR. *(V.O.)* Two and a half.

JUDY. Shit! So what do we do, eighty-six it?

LIBERACE. And the part about the mother? Less Agnes Moorehead, more Marjorie Main.

DIRECTOR. *(V.O.)* Afraid so.

JUDY. I hope you're happy. Your cockamamie story just cost me five grand in sets and costumes that no one will ever see. And by the way, you weren't booked for a guest shot. You're a walk-on. What's next?

DIRECTOR. *(V.O.)* "Life of the Party." Thirty seconds.

NIXON. *(rising)* Well! I guess I'll be going.

JUDY. You're not going anywhere. Mother's got an idea. The only way to save my show is to save your act. Now, can you do anything that might be considered remotely entertaining?

NIXON. I've got plenty of other inspiring, real-life stories.

JUDY. No! I don't want to hear one more word about real life. I've tried it, believe me, darling. It doesn't play.

*(**NIXON** looks at the others who nod sagely.)*

LIBERACE. It just sort of lies there.

ETHEL. Like Ernest Borgnine.

JUDY. Oh, come on – everybody does something!

NIXON. Not me. Now, wait. On the occasion of Julie's fifth birthday, I *did* astonish the kiddies with my magic tricks.

JUDY. Are you any good?

DIRECTOR. *(V.O.)* Fifteen seconds.

JUDY. It doesn't matter. Props!

(pushing **NIXON** *offstage)*

You go with Jerry, he'll get you everything you need.

NIXON. This is exciting.

JUDY. Go!

(to Conductor)

Mort! "Life of the Party." First four choruses as is. Then give me a vamp. I'll cue Nixon, blah, blah, blah, and then cut to the final eight.

DIRECTOR. *(V.O.)* Places everyone! In five...four...three...

JUDY. Oh, my tray!

*(***JUDY*** *grabs a prop tray of crab cakes and snaps on a cocktail apron as they all assume a stage picture of stylized, suburban party-going.)*

(Music. The doorbell rings. **JUDY** *hands her tray to* **ETHEL** *and opens the door for the* **CHORUS.***)*

JUDY.
WELCOME, WELCOME!
WE HAVE BEEN EXPECTING YOU.
NOW COME INSIDE AND MAKE YOURSELVES AT HOME!

CHORUS.
THANK YOU.

JUDY.
EVERYBODY MAKE YOURSELVES AT HOME!

ALL.
THANK YOU!

(The music accelerates as Judy's guests demand more and more of her. As she takes the presents from the **CHORUS***:)*

CHORUS GIRL #1.
A LOVELY PARTY!

CHORUS BOY #1.

    YES, WELL DONE.

JUDY.

    I'M PLEASED TO HAVE YOU. JUST HAVE FUN.

LIBERACE.

    I NEED SOME TINSEL FOR THE TREE.

JUDY. *(handing him presents)*

    YOU TAKE THESE, DEAR, I'LL GO SEE.

ETHEL. *(finishing the crab cakes)*

    LOVE THE CRAB CAKES! GOT SOME MORE?

JUDY. *(seeing the empty tray)*

    I HAD A TRAY FULL.

ETHEL.

    DON'T BE SORE.

    (as **JUDY** *starts off with tray)*

    AND CHEESE AND CRACKERS, THANK YOU DEAR.

JUDY.

    JUST HOLD ON, ETHEL. TINSEL? HERE!

    (JUDY *hands the extra tinsel to* **LIBERACE,** *who's been draping it over his arm.)*

LIBERACE.

    LOOKS BETTER, DON'T YOU THINK, ON ME?

JUDY.

    I DEFINITELY WOULD AGREE.

BING.

    I SURE COULD USE SOME CHRISTMAS CHEER.

JUDY.

    EGGNOG, FRUIT PUNCH, WINE OR BEER?

BING.

    A WEE BIT STRONGER?

JUDY.

    HEAVEN SAKES! OKAY. HERE, ETHEL. HERE'S YOUR CAKES.

CHORUS BOY #2 & CHORUS GIRL #2.

    OH, JUDY, JUDY, WON'T YOU SING?

JUDY.

    I DON'T KNOW – YOUR HIGHBALL, BING.

CHORUS BOY #2.

OH, PLEASE SING "MELANCHOLY BABY."

JUDY.

WELL, A LITTLE LATER, MAYBE.

BING.

A TOAST TO JUDY, IF I MAY.

LIBERACE.

"THE HOSTEST WITH THE MOSTEST!"

ETHEL.

HEY!

CHORUS BOY #1.

SING "SWANEE!"

CHORUS GIRL #2.

"RAINBOW!"

LIBERACE.

"STORMY WEATHER!"

JUDY.

LET ME GET MYSELF TOGETHER.

CHORUS GIRLS.

"JOHNNY ONE-NOTE!"

BING.

FROM THE TOP!

JUDY.

NO!

ETHEL.

LET ME SING IT, MORTY.

JUDY.

STOP!!!

> *(The guests freeze.* **JUDY** *takes a booklet from her apron and reads:)*

JUDY.

"EVERY HOSTESS WANTS A PARTY THAT'S SUCCESSFUL.
BUT SHE DOESN'T WANT HER EVENING TO BE STRESSFUL.
SO THAT SHE GETS A BIT OF REST,
A HOSTESS VENTURES TO SUGGEST
THAT EVERY GUEST PERFORM WITH ZEST
WHATEVER TALENT THEY DO BEST!"

OTHERS. *(resuming action)* Aaaaahh! What a novel idea! You mean me? *(etc.)*

JUDY.

> *AND THEY RARELY DO PROTEST.*
> FOR...
> *ANYONE* CAN BE THE LIFE OF THE PARTY.
> ENTERTAINING ISN'T VERY HARD TO DO.
> SO WHAT IF YOU ARE BORING,
> NO TALENT'S WORTH IGNORING.
> THE LIFE OF THE PARTY...

CHORUS.

> THE LIFE OF THE PARTY!

JUDY.

> COULD VERY WELL BE YOU.

> Trust me, darlings, any one of you here can be the Belle of the Ball!

> (**JUDY** *approaches* **LIBERACE.**)

JUDY.

> NOW FOR INSTANCE, LET US TAKE A CERTAIN MAESTRO.

LIBERACE.

> *SINCERELY YOURS.*

JUDY.

> ON THE EIGHTY-EIGHTS, HE TRULY CASTS A SPELL.

CHORUS BOYS.

> *DO TELL!*

JUDY.

> BUT IN ADDITION TO HIS TICKLING THOSE IVORIES,
> HE TELLS JOKES AND TICKLES FUNNY-BONES AS WELL!

LIBERACE. I've been dating this lovely girl. And the other evening we went to a dinner party and she had on one of those new see-through dresses. I asked her if she was wearing it to be provocative and she said, "No, I just like to keep an eye on my waistline."

> *(The* **GUESTS** *laugh and applaud.)*

JUDY, BING & ETHEL.

> ANYONE CAN BE THE LIFE OF THE PARTY!

ETHEL.

IF HE CAN DO IT, YOU CAN.

LIBERACE.

WELL, MERCI BEAUCOUP!

JUDY.

JUST USE YOUR OWN INVENTION.

WHATEVER GETS ATTENTION.

JUDY & CHORUS.

AND THE LIFE OF THE PARTY...

LIBERACE & ETHEL.

THE LIFE OF THE PARTY!

JUDY.

COULD VERY WELL BE YOU!

(**JUDY** *approaches* **BING**.)

JUDY.

SAY, HAS ANYBODY SEEN AN IRISH CROONER?

BING.

HE'S SOMEWHERE "SWINGIN' ON A STAR," I UNDERSTAND.

JUDY.

I HEARD HE TRADED IN HIS GOLF CLUBS FOR A
SAXOPHONE.

BING. *(producing a saxophone)*

IS THAT A FACT?

JUDY.

AND NOW HE'S SWINGIN' IN THE BAND!

(**BING** *plays a dreadful version of "Camptown Races" on the sax. However, the guests encourage him and he gamely brings the tune to a rousing finish. Applause.*)

JUDY, LIBERACE & ETHEL.

ANYONE CAN BE THE LIFE OF THE PARTY!

JUDY.

THE GUESTS'LL BE APPLAUDING
BY THE TIME YOU'RE THROUGH.

BING.

AND AS LONG AS THEY KEEP BOOZING,
HELL, EVERYTHING'S AMUSING.

JUDY, LIBERACE & ETHEL.

THE LIFE OF THE PARTY...

BING.

BUH, BUH, BUH, BUH, BUH, BUH.

JUDY, ETHEL, LIBERACE, CHORUS.

COULD VERY WELL BE YOU!

ETHEL. MI, MI, MI MI!

(**JUDY** *approaches* **ETHEL.**)

JUDY.

GOODNESS GRACIOUS, DO I HEAR A BROADWAY BELTER?

ETHEL.

COULD BE!

JUDY.

IRVING, GEORGE AND COLE BESTOW THEIR ACCOLADES.

ETHEL.

AS WELL THEY SHOULD!

JUDY.

UPON THE STAGE SHE DEAFENS EARS,
BUT WHEN THE CURTAIN'S DOWN
SHE DISPLAYS HER *SILENT* TALENT AT CHARADES.

(**ETHEL** *silently reads from a piece of paper. Bell tone:*)

ANNOUNCER. *(V.O.)* The answer is "Gone With The Wind."

(**ETHEL** *mimes a movie camera.*)

ALL. *(ad lib)* Movie! It's a movie!

(**ETHEL** *holds up four fingers.*)

ALL. *(ad lib)* Four words, four words.

(**ETHEL** *holds up four fingers.*)

ALL. *(ad lib)* Fourth word, fourth word.

(**ETHEL** *begins spinning around the room and flapping her arms.*)

ALL. *(ad lib)* Twirling, sailing, flying, tornado, it's a twister.

BING. "God Is My Co-Pilot!"

(*Disgusted,* **ETHEL** *glares and then mimics a flirtatious southern belle.*)

LIBERACE. "A Guy Named Joe!"

*(The last straw. **ETHEL** mimes a hoop skirt and advances toward them.)*

JUDY. "The Bride of Frankenstein!"

*(**ETHEL** angrily stamps her foot.)*

ETHEL. Aww, nuts! I'm no good at this.

ALL. *(ad lib)* Come on, you're doing great, etc.

ETHEL. I'm lousy at silent bits.

JUDY. Ethel, please.

ETHEL. Forget it.

JUDY. You're among friends.

ETHEL. Frankly, Judy, I don't give a damn!

ALL. "Gone With The Wind!"

CHORUS GIRLS.

(singing "Tara's Theme")

AAAHHH!

(Applause and congratulations.)

ALL.

ANYONE CAN BE THE LIFE OF THE PARTY!

JUDY.

BE A CLOWN!

CHORUS BOYS.

PLAY HAMLET!

BING.

DO THE OL' SOFT SHOE!

ETHEL.

SING "MAMMIE" A CAPELLA!

LIBERACE.

DO BRANDO AND YELL "STELLA!"

ALL.

THE LIFE OF THE PARTY...

*(**NIXON** enters, dressed in a top hat and gaudy magician's cape.)*

NIXON.

THE LIFE OF THE PARTY!

(The music stops.)

JUDY. *(recovering)*

Uh...well...

IT MIGHT AS WELL BE YOU.

*(The music returns, tentative, as **JUDY** improvises new lyrics.)*

JUDY.

SO I HEAR OUR NEXT GUEST LOVES A GRAND OLD PARTY.

NIXON. Do I go now?

JUDY. No.

YOU MAY WONDER HOW A V.P. GETS HIS KICKS.

NIXON. Should I begin?

JUDY.

NOT YET, DEAR,

LET ME INTRODUCE YOU, IF I MAY.

HERE HE IS FOLKS, WITH HIS BAG OF MAGIC TRICKS...

Ladies and gentlemen, uh, "Milhouse the Magnificent!"

(fanfare)

NIXON. And now, to amaze you all with a mystifying act of prestidigitation, I'll need a ten-dollar bill.

*(**NIXON** gets a ten-dollar bill from an **AUDIENCE MEMBER**.)*

NIXON. And so, with your kind permission, I shall transform this ten-dollar bill into one-dollar bills.

(He removes his top hat, revealing a swami's turban underneath, and places the ten-dollar bill in the hat.)

NIXON. Hocus pocus.

*(Drumroll. **NIXON** reaches into the hat but finds nothing. He holds it horizontally. Nothing. Finally, he turns it upside down over **JUDY**'s metal serving tray. Change trickles out of the hat. **JUDY** counts the change.)*

JUDY. Thirty-nine cents. Where's the rest of it?

NIXON. Taxes!

(Fanfare! The music accelerates.)

JUDY. Richard, give that man his money!

CHORUS BOY #1 & CHORUS GIRL #1.

THERE'S REALLY NOTHING TO IT.

CHORUS BOY #2 & CHORUS GIRL #2.

AND ANYONE CAN DO IT.

BING.

FROM SINGERS COOL AND CLASSY...

ETHEL.

TO DIVAS BOLD AND BRASSY...

LIBERACE.

FROM GRANDIOSE MUSICIANS...

NIXON.

TO SWEATING POLITICIANS...

ALL (EXCEPT JUDY).

THE LIFE OF THE PARTY...

(JUDY *plays "The Life Of The Party" on a kazoo.)*

ALL. *(pointing to* **JUDY***)*

COULD VERY WELL BE *YOU*!

(applause)

JUDY. Take five, everybody, you've earned it.

(to audience)

I've got a very special friend I'd like you to meet.

(The others go offstage as **JUDY** *crosses downstage right to the piano-bar.)*

I hope I can persuade him to say hello. He's really rather shy. Punch? Punch, darling!

(A NOISE from below the piano bar.)

JUDY. *(cont.)* What's going on down there?

PUNCH. *(off)* I'm late to work.

JUDY. Work? Punch, who works on Christmas Eve?

(Music. **PUNCH**, *a goofy dragon hand-puppet, pops up with a mailman's hat and a bag of letters.)*

PUNCH. A mailman! Neither rain nor snow nor gloom of night shall keep me from my appointed rounds. I hope it isn't nippy out.

JUDY. Now where are you delivering all these letters?

PUNCH. Let's see. This one's going to the North Pole. And so's this one. And this one is, too!

JUDY. Punch, do you know what these are?

PUNCH. They're awfully heavy. Chain letters?

JUDY. These are children's letters to Santa Claus.

PUNCH. Oh!

JUDY. But Santa's getting ready to take off and deliver his toys right now. You'll never make it to the North Pole in time.

PUNCH. The poor children! I feel simply terrible. Oh, Judy! What am I going to do?

JUDY. Goodness sakes, oh, dear…I don't know.

(music under)

JUDY. But whenever I'm in trouble I take a deep breath and look way up in the sky.

PUNCH. Over the rainbow?

JUDY. Well, when you're really in trouble, sometimes you have to look even further.

(singing)

FAR, FAR AWAY
IN MOONFALL'S GLEAM,
A GOLDEN STAR IS GLISTENING.
AND WHEN I PRAY,
THROUGH STRANGE AS IT MAY SEEM,
THAT STAR SO VERY FAR AWAY IS LISTENING.

ANGEL STAR,
GLOWING EVERY EVENING SOFT AND BRIGHT,
YOU HAVE ALWAYS BEEN MY GUIDING LIGHT
WHEN I HAVE LOST MY WAY.

ANGEL STAR,
SITTING IN THE SKY IN WONDROUS VIEW,
SHINE FOR ME TONIGHT SO I MIGHT FOLLOW YOU.

SOMETIMES THE ROAD IS CLEAR,
BUT THEN STORMS APPEAR ON HIGH.
DARKNESS ALL AROUND
AND I AM LEFT TO ROAM.

BUT WHAT HAVE I TO FEAR?
NO, I MERELY SAY A PRAYER.
SOON MY FRIENDLY STAR IS THERE
TO LEAD ME HOME.

OH...
ANGEL STAR,
SMILE ON ME IF YOU WOULD BE SO KIND.
SHOW ME WHERE TO SEEK
AND I SHALL FIND
WHAT I SHOULD SEE.
MY ANGEL STAR, PLEASE SHINE FOR ME.

(**JUDY** *strains to listen as the star "speaks" to her with twinkly music.*)

What?...Are you sure?

PUNCH. *(worried)* Uh, Judy?

JUDY. *(to star)* Oh, yes. And thank you!

(to **PUNCH***)*

Punch, I have it on very good authority that Santa Claus never misses one of my shows. If you read those letters on the air, he'll make sure the children get their presents.

PUNCH. He will? Hooray!

JUDY.

IF YOU ARE
SEARCHING FOR AN ANSWER HEAVEN-SENT...
IF YOU LONG TO KNOW THE PATH YOU'RE MEANT
TO TRAVEL ON,
MAKE A WISH UPON
YOUR LUCKY...

PUNCH.
> LOVELY...

JUDY & PUNCH.
> ANGEL STAR!

PUNCH. Judy, you're so wonderful.

JUDY. Oh, stop.

> *(They kiss. Applause.)*

JUDY. I think we're going to need help with all this mail.

PUNCH. I do, too. I can't read.

JUDY. Then I've got the perfect person!

PUNCH. Do they know anything about the post office?

JUDY. She's America's First Lady of Letters.

PUNCH. Does she like boys and girls?

JUDY. I should say so. She's the author of "Toys In The Attic" and "The Children's Hour." Ladies and gentlemen, Miss Lillian Hellman.

> *(Applause. Music.* **LILLIAN HELLMAN** *enters; tweedy, taciturn and armed with an ever-present cigarette.)*

LILLIAN. Hello, Judy.

JUDY. Lilly. And this is my good friend, Punch.

> *(***PUNCH** *mugs.* **LILLIAN** *regards him blankly.)*

JUDY. Darling, would you mind reading a little something for us?

LILLIAN. I thought I'd begin with a scene from my prize-winning play, "The Little Foxes." This is a family drama about the corrosive effects of corruption and greed.

JUDY. Oh, no no. We need you to read something else.

LILLIAN. Like what?

PUNCH. Children's letters to Santa.

LILLIAN. You've got to be kidding.

PUNCH. But Judy said you're America's First Lady of Letters.

LILLIAN. I write 'em, I don't read 'em.

> *(peering behind piano-bar)*

Who's in there?

JUDY. Look – uh, darling – we're in quite a predicament.

LILLIAN. So I see.

(She sighs, takes a letter and reads.)

"Dear Santa. My name is Chris and this year I want a hot pink go-cart. It's okay if you can't afford it, just charge it like Daddy does."

PUNCH. Do you think Chris is a boy or a girl?

LILLIAN. I think Chris is a capitalist.

JUDY. Uh, this next letter is from Debbie. Here's her picture and she says she's seven years old.

LILLIAN. *(looks at picture)* She's ten if she's a day.

(reading)

"Dear Santa. Hi, it's me, Debbie. I want a Betsy-Wetsy doll. If you promise to bring me a Betsy-Wetsy doll, I promise to leave you some milk and cookies."

JUDY. Isn't that adorable?

LILLIAN. No, Judy, it's not, it's appalling. Your "Santa Claus" is just a merchandising gimmick for big business to sell worthless junk to American children who don't need it.

*(**LILLIAN** walks out of the television spotlight and appeals to the studio audience.)*

LILLIAN. *(cont.)* The people of China, Africa, and yes, Russia, don't have the luxury of choosing highfalutin presents out of the Sears & Roebuck catalog because they're starving for hope or food or both.

JUDY. I think we've got time for one more.

PUNCH. I'll get it.

*(**PUNCH** disappears. **JUDY** turns angrily to **LILLIAN** in sotto voice:)*

JUDY. What the hell are you doing?

LILLIAN. You tell me. Why did you invite me here?

JUDY. It's the culture spot. You're supposed to represent culture. Like Carl Sandburg or Pearl S. Buck. Punch, we're waiting for that letter.

(Lighting special as **PUNCH** *returns with the letter in his mouth.)*

(But unseen by **JUDY** *and* **LILLIAN**, *a skeletal hand forces* **PUNCH** *back down, strangling him.)*

LILLIAN. Now look. Culture's one thing. But all this Merry Christmas crap is *forcing* struggling families *down* into debt, systematically *strangled* by an economic system that's wringing the life out of the proletariat –

(Suddenly, **PUNCH** *is flung from behind the piano-bar and lands on the floor at* **JUDY**'s *feet.)*

JUDY. Punch?

(She nudges the lifeless puppet with her shoe.)

JUDY. He's…he's dead? Cut. CUT!

*(***JUDY** *picks up* **PUNCH**. *An abrupt light change signals a station break.)*

JUDY. This isn't happening…this isn't happening…

*(***BING** *[drinking],* **ETHEL** *[eating] and* **LIBERACE** *[wearing the Sailor's hat], appear from the wings.)*

BING. *(handing* **JUDY** *his drink)* Settle down now, sweetpea.

JUDY. Settle down! A puppet has been murdered!

LIBERACE. Murdered!

ETHEL. For Pete's sake, Judy, what's the big deal?

JUDY. I've put everything I've got – blood – into this show and someone's trying to ruin it!

BING. Maybe they caught it on the time delay.

JUDY. Do you think so? I completely forgot…

DIRECTOR. *(V.O.)* Hold on, Judy, we're checking…yep, we caught it. We're back in business.

JUDY. Oh, thank God!

(to audience)

I apologize, ladies and gentlemen. Please bear with us.

(to guests)

Listen, everybody, let's relax. Calm down.

(**JUDY** *sees* **LILLIAN** *staring across the stage at* **NIXON**.)

JUDY. Lilly, what's wrong? You look like you've seen a ghost.

LILLIAN. What the hell's he doing here?

JUDY. The vice-president? Why?

LILLIAN. Why do you think I'm stuck here talking to a puppet? Because Tricky Dick and his Washington witch-hunt gang killed my career in this town.

JUDY. But he's really...he did some marvelous magic tricks. You know, making things disappear?

LILLIAN. Yeah. Like the First Amendment. Hey, Nixon! Remember me?

NIXON. Uh, I, uh –

LILLIAN. The name's Hellman.

NIXON. Oh, yes. The condiment heiress. Hellman's Mayonnaise.

LILLIAN. No! *Lillian* Hellman!

NIXON. A-ha! Here's your 'Life of the Party,' Miss Garland. The *Communist* party!

JUDY. She's not a Communist.

NIXON. She's as red as the nose on Rudolph The Red-Nosed Reindeer. And the very idea that you'd give this radical a forum to infiltrate the innocent hearts and minds of America's children –

LILLIAN. Can it, Dick, we're off the air. And besides, you won. You brought nothing but bad trouble to good people and for what?

NIXON. I did it for my country!

LILLIAN. You did it for publicity.

DIRECTOR. *(V.O.)* Thirty seconds.

JUDY. Now, look you two. I don't have time for ancient history. And I don't care who did what to whom. This is Christmas, goddammit! And you are guests in my home. Now Bing and I are going to sing a romantic number and while we do, I want the two of you sit down and shut up!

(**NIXON** *and* **LILLIAN** *start to argue.*)

JUDY. DON'T – FUCK – WITH – DOROTHY!

*(They grudgingly retreat. **JUDY** and **BING** take their places, sharing sheet music with a snowman on the cover.)*

DIRECTOR. *(V.O.)* …in five, four, three…

(MUSIC)

JUDY.

OL' JACK FROST IS COMIN' ROUND.
SO BRACE FOR CHILLY WEATHER.

LILLIAN. Worm.

NIXON. Red.

JUDY.

BEFORE A SNOWFLAKE HITS THE GROUND,
LET'S BUNDLE UP TOGETHER.

LILLIAN. Liar!

NIXON. Pinko!

BING.

WE'LL KEEP WITHIN OUR COZY DEN
LIKE BEARS IN HIBERNATION…

LILLIAN. Fascist villain!!!

NIXON. Commie bitch!!!

(They attack each other.)

JUDY. Mort, stop the music! Uh, folks, I've just discovered we've got two old friends right here on this show. As you can see, they can hardly keep their hands off each other.

*(She pulls the stricken **NIXON** and **LILLIAN** into the light.)*

JUDY. So, Bing, I think you and I should bow out and let these two lovebirds take the spotlight.

BING. You're the teacher.

(Unknown to anyone the sheet music has been transformed and now features a skull wearing a top hat.)

NIXON. You're not going to leave us alone, are you?

JUDY. You're not alone, Dick. You've got the audience and the orchestra…and twenty-eight million Americans.

LILLIAN. Look, a puppet's one thing, but I don't know if I can –

JUDY. For crying out loud, Lilly, I'm not asking you to name names. Just sing.

*(**JUDY** and **BING** leave. A pause. Music intro. **LILLIAN** and **NIXON** grudgingly sing:)*

LILLIAN.
OL' JACK FROST IS COMIN' ROUND.
SO BRACE FOR CHILLY WEATHER.
BEFORE A SNOWFLAKE HITS THE GROUND,
LET'S BUNDLE UP TOGETHER.

NIXON.
WE'LL KEEP WITHIN OUR COZY DEN
LIKE BEARS IN HIBERNATION.
AND BE CONTENT…

BOTH.
…OUR WINTER SPENT
EXPRESSING ADORATION.

NIXON.
DECEMBER'S ROAR IS AT OUR DOOR.
WE'RE SNUGGLED SAFE INSIDE.

LILLIAN.
THE FIRE'S AGLOW.
THE LIGHTS ARE LOW.
AND ME, I'M STARRY-EYED.

NIXON.
ROMANCE IS NEW TO ME, I FEAR.
I PUT TO YOU THE QUESTION, DEAR –
ARE YOU NOW OR HAVE YOU EVER BEEN…
IN LOVE?

LILLIAN.
I MIGHT SAY "NAY" WITHOUT DELAY.

NIXON.
DON'T WASTE MY TIME WITH GAMES!

LILLIAN.

OR I MIGHT PURR,

"I'M GUILTY, SIR."

NIXON.

CONFESS!

AND GIVE ME NAMES!

BOTH.

THIS NIGHT DIVINE COULD BE SO FINE,

LILLIAN.

BUT ALL HE'S THINKING OF...

BOTH.

IS SHE NOW OR HAS SHE EVER

BEEN IN LOVE?

(In spite of themselves, **NIXON** *and* **LILLIAN** *begin to enjoy the number – and each other.)*

LILLIAN.

WHEN YOU'RE HOLDING ME TIGHT...

NIXON.

IT IS A DELIGHT!

LILLIAN.

LET THE RECORD SHOW IT FEELS SO RIGHT.

NIXON.

IT WAS LOVE AT FIRST SIGHT!

LILLIAN.

WELL, NOT QUITE.

NIXON.

AND IN SPITE OF THE FACT YOU'RE A RED,

YOU GO TO MY HEAD.

(music under)

Miss Hellman, you stand accused of being a highly stimulating woman.

LILLIAN. Why, thank you, Mr. Chairman. Am I still under oath?

NIXON. No, but you are under the mistletoe. Truth to tell, Lillian, I always thought you were a "little fox."

LILLIAN. Come now, Richard. Do you have any evidence to support your claim?

NIXON. Pucker up, baby and I'll show you Exhibit A.

*(**NIXON** proffers a kiss. **LILLIAN** coyly declines. Music builds.)*

LILLIAN.

I'VE KNOWN SOME PRICKS IN POLITICS,
BUT YOU I CAN'T RESIST.

NIXON.

I WON'T OBJECT!
AND I SUSPECT...

LILLIAN.

WHAT?

NIXON.

YOU'RE ON MY CHRISTMAS LIST.

LILLIAN.

YOU AND YOUR LISTS!

NIXON.

A COLD WAR'S DUE.

LILLIAN.

CAREERS ARE THROUGH.

BOTH.

STILL YOU I DO ADORE.
ASK ME, "ARE YOU NOW?"
I'LL SAY, "FOREVERMORE!"

NIXON.

LET THE BLIZZARD WHIRL.

LILLIAN.

AND THANK SAINT NICK.

NIXON.

I GOT THE GIRL!

LILLIAN.

AND I GOT DICK!

BOTH.

UNTIL NOW, WE'VE NEVER BEEN IN LOVE...
BEFORE!!!

NIXON. *Oh, Yes!*

> *(Applause.* **JUDY** *and the others welcome* **NIXON** *and* **LILLIAN** *back to the living room set.)*

ETHEL. You kids are headed for the top of the bill!

LIBERACE. Steve and Eydie, watch out!

NIXON. I don't know about that. I'm not much of a threat to Der Bingle here.

BING. *(raising his glass in salute)* Competition's getting mighty stiff.

JUDY. Lilly, I had no idea you were so musical.

LILLIAN. Well, you know I wrote "Candide."

JUDY. What?

LILLIAN. "Candide?" Skip it.

> *(The doorbell rings; this time in a minor key.* **JUDY** *reacts, puzzled.)*

JUDY. Goodness…I guess she's early. Listen everybody, I've got a big surprise for you – one of the most glamorous stars in the history of Hollywood. She's starred in so many pictures, I can't begin to remember them all, but I know I've seen every single one. Ladies and gentlemen, Academy Award winner, Miss Joan Crawford!

> *(Applause as* **JUDY** *throws open the door to reveal —* **DEATH***! The tall figure is shrouded in black, his long, skeletal hands clutching a scythe. Green fog swirls about his feet and ominous music is heard.* **DEATH** *emits an echoing shriek of doom.)*

JUDY. Joan?

> *(Stricken,* **JUDY** *turns to the camera.)*

JUDY. We'll be right back.

> *(Musics and blackout)*

End of Act One

ACT TWO

(Lights up. Ominous music. **DEATH** *shrieks again.)*

JUDY. Is this some kind of joke? Is this a surprise? Because I HATE surprises! George! Where the hell is everybody?

STAGE MANAGER. *(V.O.) (through a field of static)* Sorry, Judy, we can't find him. Look…we've got a technical…the electricals have gone haywire up here…

JUDY. Up there? What about down here?

STAGE MANAGER. *(V.O.)* Thirty seconds.

JUDY. Thirty seconds? To what? I can't put this on the air.

BING. Now, hold on Judy – he's got you going with the oldest trick in the book.

JUDY. A trick!

BING. I taped a special over at Desilu and who do you think walked in dressed up like the Easter Bunny?

JUDY. Who?

BING. Sinatra!

JUDY. Frank did that?

BING. You play along with the gag and I guarantee that old spook'll turn out to be Frank or Dean or maybe even Jerry Lewis.

JUDY. Oh, God, I hope not.

STAGE MANAGER. And in five…four…

*(***DEATH*** *sits in the star spot. Music. Lights up.* **JUDY** *snaps on a nervous smile.)*

JUDY. We're back. And welcome to "What's My Line." As you can see we've been joined by a rather mysterious stranger. So let's find out who he is, shall we?

*(***JUDY*** *sits next to* **DEATH** *and gestures for the other guests to gather round. They warily comply.)*

JUDY. *(cont.)* You know, when you first came on you gave us quite a start, all decked out in that Christmas Carol get-up.

LIBERACE. Are you the Ghost of Christmas Yet To Come?

(DEATH shakes his head.)

JUDY. He's not fictional. Though you certainly scared the Dickens out of us. Now, are you a world-famous singer who's known as "The Chairman of the Board?"

(DEATH shakes his head. JUDY turns nervously to BING.)

BING. Are you the Eye-talian crooner that sang the one about the pizza pie?

(DEATH shakes his head.)

JUDY. You're not Jerry Lewis, are you?

(DEATH shakes his head.)

(relieved) That's something. Well, whoever you are, you've stumped the stars. Who are you?

DEATH. *(an unworldly voice)* I – Am – Death.

(A moment of stunned silence. ETHEL harrumphs:)

ETHEL. You're telling me!

BING. Come on now, pally, enough trick or treat. Who are you?

DEATH. I – AM – DEATH!

(to JUDY)

And I have come for you.

(JUDY freezes but quickly rallies.)

JUDY. Of course, you have, darling. But I'm in the middle of a party and I'm expecting another guest any second.

(prompting booth)

In fact, she's just about to ring my doorbell…right now!

(A fast "ding-dong" doorbell. JUDY rushes to the door.)

Miss Joan Crawford!

*(Music. Everyone, even **DEATH**, applauds as **JOAN CRAWFORD** grandly enters, wearing a glittering evening gown. **JOAN** heads straight downstage center to the audience, ignoring **JUDY**.)*

*(The guests on the sofa, including **DEATH**, rise and move down to accomodate **JOAN**.)*

JUDY. Joan, darling, Merry Christmas.

JOAN. Merry Christmas to you, Judy. Don't you look festive? And Happy Holidays to your guests and to all my fans watching in each and every country around the world tonight, thank you for that warm welcome.

JUDY. Can I offer you a beverage?

JOAN. I never say "no" to a refreshing Pepsi-Cola.

*(**JUDY** obligingly offers her a pre-set bottle of Pepsi-Cola with a straw. **JOAN** takes a sip.)*

JOAN. Pepsi-Cola hits the spot.

(reading the bottle)

Twelve full ounces? That's a lot!

JUDY. Yeah. Well, I hear you've just finished making a marvelous new picture for Fox.

JOAN. Why, yes indeed, I have. It's called "The Best Of Everything." And you know, Judy, that's my special wish for all the children of the world this blessed season. "The Best Of Everything."

LILLIAN. Oh, brother!

JUDY. Speaking of children, where are your two adorable little ones?

JOAN. Christopher and Christina? They're at home watching their Mommie Dearest on television. Hello, children.

*(**JOAN** beams into the camera, waves warmly and then abruptly points threateningly.)*

JUDY. I'll bet they can't wait for you to get home so they can open their presents.

JOAN. We don't open our presents on Christmas Eve, Judy. We open our bible instead. And you know, I think if more families did just that, we wouldn't have all these "teen troubles" we have today. No, Judy, we open our presents on Christmas morning. I allow the children to play with their toys all day long. And then, they choose one toy to keep for their very own and all the rest are donated to the needy little ones at the Beverly Hills Orphans Asylum.

JUDY. Speaking of the…Bible, I understand you're going to read us a little something.

JOAN. It's our favorite tradition in the Crawford home. The story of His birth.

JUDY. Whose birth? Oh, Him! Divine. Joan Crawford, everybody.

(*JUDY leads the applause as* **JOAN** *crosses to a lectern which holds a massive white bible. Music.*)

JOAN. In the days of Caesar Augustus, a decree went out that every person should return to their place of birth so that a census might be taken. The road from Galilee was a long and difficult one. But the Virgin Mary, great with child, put her trust in the bronzed, muscular arms of her faithful husband. "Thank you, Joseph," said Mary as he lifted her onto an ill-tempered donkey, "you're a saint."

That night, in the little town of Bethlehem, Joseph sought lodging for them at a shabby Inn on the wrong side of the tracks. Suddenly, the door flung open and the rough-looking but not unattractive, Innkeeper barked, "There no room at the Inn. Scram!" Defeated, Joseph turned to go. Just like a man. So Mary stepped forward. "I want a room. I'm a plain, simple woman who's been riding all day on the back of a jackass named Trouble and I'm tired."

Before the Innkeeper could slam the door in her face, Mary grabbed his bronzed, muscular arm and pleaded, "I'll wash dishes, I'll scrub floors. And, yes, as God is my judge, I'll even…if I must…bake pies."

(DEATH turns to JOAN in disbelief.)

And lo the Innkeeper brought them to a manger where he made for her a bed of straw. And with that, Mary lay down among the ox and the ass and the lion and the lamb and that place was a pig sty! Dirt. Filth. Animal shit. From *animals!* Too tired to clean, Mary? Try riding a jackass named Jack Warner all day long. I'd have scrubbed that place from top to bottom before MY head hit the pillow! And really, Mary. Nine months pregnant *and* a virgin?

(shrugging)

You're the boss.

(DEATH rises ominously.)

Nevertheless, a child was born and it came to pass that three wise men brought him gifts of gold, frankincense and myrrh. And Mary allowed Jesus to play with his gifts all day long and then he chose one to keep as his very own...

(JUDY gestures "cut" but JOAN doesn't see her.)

...while all the rest were donated to the precious little ones at the Bethlehem Orphans Asylum.

(DEATH raises his skeletal hand.)

DEATH. Silence!

(The bible bursts into flames. JOAN screams.)

JUDY. George! Security! Props! Joan, darling, I'm terribly sorry.

(The others put out the fire and remove the lectern as JOAN turns furiously toward DEATH.)

JOAN. Listen, you third rate Houdini! I'm the star and I've got the star's spot, so just who the hell do you think you are?

DEATH. I – Am – Death.

JOAN. YOU'RE – AN – AMATEUR!

(DEATH takes a step backwards.)

JUDY. *(now frantic)* I've been thinking and you know, thinking helps, it really does. And I've often…thought, wouldn't it be marvelous if we could jump onto a magical trolley and journey back to our favorite Christmases of yesteryear?

(She snaps her fingers to count off the beats.)

JUDY. One, two, three…

(no music)

JUDY. Mort? I know I'm changing the program…everybody ready? Let's try it again, shall we?

(She counts off the beats again. No music.)

JUDY.
WITH MY HIGH-STARCHED COLLAR

DEATH. Judy…

JUDY.
AND MY HIGH-TOP SHOES

DEATH. Judy…

JUDY.
AND MY HAIR PILED HIGH UPON MY…
What? What!

DEATH. There is no more to sing about. The time is at hand.

JUDY. No. Bing, you make him go away.

(BING *approaches* **DEATH.)**

BING. All right, son, you've had your fun. Just run along now.

(DEATH *moans but doesn't move.)*

LIBERACE. I think a job like this calls for a *real* man.

BING. Like who, you?

(an ugly laugh)

You big, fat sissy.

LIBERACE. Aww, go beat your kids you jug-eared old drunk.

ETHEL. Spread out! You slobs couldn't give the hook to Ted Mack.

(to **DEATH***)*

Say buddy, you sure scared the wad out of Judy. Look at the poor kid, shaking like a leaf. So that's your act – "Chill 'em and kill 'em!"

(confidentially offering him theatre tickets)

Say, have you seen, "Sound of Music?"

(DEATH *is tempted, but declines.)*

LILLIAN. You can't bargain with a bully. You've got to stand your ground. You've got to dig in your heels. You've got to hit them with both barrels.

JOAN. *(dramatically)* Get out! Get your things out of here before I throw them into the street and you with them. Get out before I kill you!

(DEATH *doesn't move.)*

JOAN. *(a shrug)* It worked in "Mildred Pierce."

DEATH. *(turning to* **JUDY***)* I have come for you.

ETHEL. Get the wax out, Mac, she ain't going no place.

DEATH. I have come for *all* of you.

(a deadly pause)

LIBERACE. Uh-oh.

ETHEL. All of us? What's this joker talking about, Judy?

DEATH. You have strayed.

BING. I strayed a time or two in my day but I always came clean with the little woman, so what's all the hub-bub, bub?

DEATH. You misunderstand. I am bound to return your souls.

BING. Then I'll tell you what I *do* understand. I've got a contract here that says I'm doing a show with Judy Garland at CBS on Christmas Eve, 1959.

DEATH. This is not the year nineteen hundred and fifty-nine.

(DEATH *waves his hand. The lights flicker and mysterious music is heard. A chill passes through the room.)*

JOAN. That's absolutely ridiculous. Of course, it's 1959. It's Christmas Eve.

LIBERACE. After the show, I'm having midnight supper with that young serviceman.

NIXON. I'm going out for a constitutional with Checkers.

JOAN. And I'm having drinks at the Mocambo with Forrest Tucker.

(**DEATH** *points at the record album.* **ETHEL** *begins to remember.*)

ETHEL. Say, something very funny's going on here. You know, I never made a Hawaiian record. I didn't even go to Hawaii in '59. I was in Jamaica.

JUDY. I thought Lena Horne was in Jamaica.

ETHEL. That was a show, Judy.

JUDY. Oh…

(*The* **OTHERS** *begin to remember.*)

BING. Hold on now, Christmas '59, I was up at the ranch.

LIBERACE. Come to think of it, I was playing a benefit at the Stardust with Marilyn Maxwell.

NIXON. Pat and I were at Camp David with Ike and Mamie.

JOAN. I was living in New York. I'd just lost Al.

BING. My old noggin' seems to playing tricks on me.

NIXON. I believe we're all the victims of a Communist brain-washing experiment.

LILLIAN. You would.

LIBERACE. What about Judy?

JOAN. In 1959, you were…you were…

ETHEL. I remember! You were fat! Remember how fat you were?

LIBERACE. You were in the hospital. It was in *Variety*.

NIXON. I believe it was in all the papers.

JOAN. I felt terrible.

BING. I sent you some flowers. A big bunch of…of…

JUDY. Gladiolas.

(candidly)

I was in Doctor's Hospital in New York. My liver had swollen to four times its size. The doctors drained five gallons of poison out of my body. They said I'd never walk again. Never work again. I showed them. But I had to take a raincheck on Christmas that year. So here we are.

ETHEL. And where the hell's that?

*(**JUDY** looks at **DEATH** who answers gently:)*

DEATH. You are all dead.

(They all stop and look at each other, aghast.)

ETHEL. Dead? I ain't dead! I'm booked through the summer of '61. I'm in the biggest hit of my life. Things look swell. Things look great. Gonna have the whole world on a...

(giving in)

Dead, huh? Well, it's not like we all died in '59? Is it?

DEATH. No. You die in the year nineteen hundred and eighty-four.

ETHEL. That's more like it. Gives me plenty of time to star in some new hit shows on Broadway.

DEATH. There will be no new hit shows. Revivals. Television. Sit-coms.

ETHEL. *(stricken)* Sit-coms!

DEATH. "That Girl." "Batman." "The Love Boat."

ETHEL. Aww, what the hell. At least I won the Tony for "Gypsy." Right?

*(**DEATH** points to the record album. **ETHEL** looks, screams and drops it. **LIBERACE** picks it up.)*

BING. What is it, Lee?

*(**LIBERACE** displays the album which has transformed into...)*

LIBERACE. Mary Martin in "The Sound of Music."

(They all take one step back from DEATH *except* ETHEL, *who explodes:)*

ETHEL. Goddamn it!

(then, resigned)

Well, you can't buck a nun.

(aside to DEATH*)*

You know she's a dyke?

*(*DEATH *nods. He turns invitingly to the others.)*

NIXON. Just tell me this: Do I become President of the United States of America?

*(*DEATH *nods.)*

NIXON. Hot diggity! I beat that son-of-a-bitch, Jack Kennedy!

DEATH. No. He wins.

*(*LILLIAN *chortles.)*

DEATH. You win eight years later. Then you're re-elected in a landslide.

*(*LILLIAN *stops laughing.* NIXON *claps his hands.)*

NIXON. I guess you'll have Dick Nixon to kick around just a little longer.

DEATH. And then you are the first President to resign from office in disgrace.

*(*NIXON *chokes.* LILLIAN *laughs.)*

LILLIAN. This is a great party! Okay, I'll bite. How did I die?

DEATH. Ah, the celebrated author, Lillian Hellman. "Pentimento," "An Unfinished Woman," and "The Children's Hour," that marvelous morality play about the destructive power of a lie.

LILLIAN. *(sincerely)* Gee, thanks.

DEATH. Rest assured, your reputation will survive as one of our finest writers of fiction.

LILLIAN. Fiction! What do you mean, "fiction?" My autobiographies were acclaimed as frank, forthright –

DEATH. Fiction. You cast yourself as the invincible heroine of your own life with your contemporaries as bumbling supporting players.

LILLIAN. But it was *my* story. And I had every right to tell it the way I saw fit.

DEATH. Was your interpretation really worth the lies you sowed to achieve it?

(Startled, **LILLIAN** *meekly asks:)*

LILLIAN. So how did I die?

DEATH. As you lived. Brilliant. Misunderstood. Angry.

*(***LILLIAN** *sits, stunned. A beat.)*

BING. I don't know about you gloomy Gusses, but when it's my time to take the final bow, I want to do it with a birdie on the eighteenth hole.

DEATH. You did. On a golf course in Spain. You won the game. You won almost everything. On earth.

BING. Luck of the Irish. Say, what do you mean, "on earth?" Aren't we on earth?

DEATH. Perhaps. But soon you will be…"Going My Way."

ETHEL. Where are we going? The Pearly Gates?

LIBERACE. We're not going to Hell, are we?

DEATH. Your destination is the void in between. Where you shall return to await your judgment.

ETHEL. Judgment?

LIBERACE. Hi. I think there's been a terrible mistake.

DEATH. Ah, yes. The young man with the candelabra. There has been no mistake.

LIBERACE. But I was good to my mother. I always played an extra encore. And I won the Good Samaritan Award from the Las Vegas Casino Association – two years in a row.

DEATH. In vain, in vain…

ETHEL. Face the music, maestro, it's curtains.

LIBERACE. All right, so I'm dead. Fiddlesticks. I just pray I didn't linger.

(a beat)

LIBERACE. Oh, don't tell me I lingered.

DEATH. You died from a disease known to afflict homosexuals.

LIBERACE. *(a nervous laugh)* What's that got to do with me?

DEATH. Oh, Mary, don't ask.

LIBERACE. But...I'm Mr. Showmanship.

DEATH. Alas, the show is over.

JOAN. Pardon me, I'm Joan Crawford of Hollywood, USA – and I'd like to ask you just one question.

DEATH. *(pronounced 'Le Sewer')* Yes, Miss Le Sueur.

JOAN. What?

DEATH. Lucille Le Sueur. Of San Antonio, Texas.

JOAN. That's "le *sir*." I'm not frightened of your judgment. Every time I step before the cameras, I'm judged by millions. What I want to know is this: Do I continue to star in motion pictures?

*(**DEATH** nods. **JOAN** turns to the others with smug satisfaction. Then:)*

DEATH. "Straight-Jacket." "Berserk." "Trog."

JOAN. Oh, yes... "Trog." Well, at least I'll have the perpetual love and loyalty of my children.

*(**DEATH** deadpans the audience.)*

JOAN. But...I've been a wonderful mother. True, there *were* rumors. It's not as if I'm some kind of monster.

DEATH. *(softly)* But you are, Joan. You are.

BING. Hey, big fella – lay off the little lady. Nobody's perfect. And I'd like to hear one good reason why we're all being judged!

*(The others rise, joining **BING** in protest. **DEATH** sighs. Music.)*

DEATH. *(to **BING**)* Too cold.

*(to **LILLIAN**)*

Too hot.

(to ETHEL*)*

Too loud.

(to LIBERACE*)*

Too weird.

(to JOAN*)*

Too much.

(to JUDY*)*

Too good.

NIXON. How true!

DEATH. Two-faced!

JUDY. *(exploding)* I can't stand anymore of this!

(attacking DEATH*)*

Get get out of my home!

(bursting into tears)

You weren't invited!

*(*DEATH *calmly hands* JUDY *a cold invitation.)*

JUDY. But how did you...? Someone's circled the address. And there's some writing here.

ETHEL. What's it say, kid?

JUDY. "See you there. R.N."

DEATH. What an awkward situation.

(They all look incriminatingly at NIXON*.)*

NIXON. What are you looking at me for?

LIBERACE. "See you there. R.N.?"

NIXON. Perhaps there's a registered nurse in the audience.

ETHEL. You're gonna need one.

NIXON. *(to* DEATH*)* I could use a little help here.

DEATH. I have none to give.

NIXON. But we had a deal!

LILLIAN. I knew it!

JUDY. You bastard! You sold us out!

BING. Why'd you turn Benedict Arnold on us?

JOAN. Judas Iscariot!

NIXON. *(to* **DEATH***)* I won that chess game, fair and square.

ETHEL. So he gets to go to Heaven?

DEATH. Not anymore.

(to **NIXON***)*

There is no winner in betrayal, Richard. Once again, you have failed your test.

NIXON. But…you promised. Mother's waiting for me!

*(***NIXON*** begins to cry.* **LILLIAN** *awkwardly comforts him.)*

DEATH. Friends. I have answered all the questions you have put before me. Now I have but one for each of you.

(a beat)

Why have you returned where none dare return?

BING. We were booked! Jeesh!

ETHEL. I came on to plug my Hawaiian album.

(to **JUDY***)*

The one I never recorded.

LIBERACE. It's always been a dream of mine to work with the great Judy Garland.

JOAN. Twentieth Century-Fox has winged me from coast to coast to promote my new picture, in Cinemascope, "The Best of Everything." And that's what I wish for you this holiday season, "The Best of Everything."

*(***DEATH*** *unleashes a shriek of exasperation that triggers an ominous rumbling. The set SHAKES and décorations fall to the floor. Silence.)*

NIXON. Judy did it! She's the mastermind behind this whole thing!

JUDY. Mastermind?

JOAN. Dick's right. You've made a horrible mess of everything.

BING. The jig's up, sister. You'd better come clean.

JUDY. Now don't you start.

LIBERACE. Oh, what a wicked web we weave when first we practice to de –

JUDY. *(cutting him off)* For Chrissakes!

JOAN. It certainly wasn't *our* idea, was it Lilly?

LILLIAN. I'm not an informer. And I won't cut my conscience to fit this year's fashion.

ETHEL. Change the record, pinko.

LILLIAN. It's not *all* her fault.

ETHEL. Hah! Do you think we'd be here if she hadn't clicked her ruby red heels together and dragged us into her big fucking comeback?

JOAN. Simmer down, Ethel.

ETHEL. And to top it off, she waltzes out looking like Tinker Bell but she's got me blown up like Tugboat Annie.

BING. Oh, Judy. Why couldn't you leave well enough alone?

JUDY. *(an outburst)* Because I couldn't! I had to do something. I'd been waiting so long. All that nothing. I just wanted to sing again.

(to **DEATH***)*

And I don't need you to tell me how I died. I remember. I was naked on a toilet with a stomach full of seconals. Now I thought about that for a long time. Was that what it all added up to? Well, I'm not going to let it. Because it wasn't enough for me.

(to others)

JUDY. *(cont.)* And it wasn't enough for you either, or you wouldn't be here. Would you? Well, would you!

(a pause…then:)

BING. I spent a long time in a dark place. Man, oh man, did I get to thinking. It seems I spent my whole life making strangers happy. And the ones I should've… cherished, well, like the song says, "You Always Hurt The One You Love."

(near tears)

BING. *(cont.)* Too late. Can't go back. So I prayed. Boy, did I pray. For someone, anybody to ask me for the smallest thing. A hand. Just something I could still give.

(to **JUDY***)*

You did.

DEATH. *(nods, pleased)* Very well. If you return with me now, your transgression shall be pardoned.

NIXON. P-pardon me, did you say p-pardoned?

*(***DEATH*** nods and gestures. The door opens.* **NIXON** *starts out – and then turns back.)*

NIXON. When the people looked at Jack Kennedy, they saw who they wanted to be. When they looked at Nixon, they saw who they were. But when I walked through that door you all seemed so happy to see *me*. I felt welcome. It was wonderful not to be alone. I'm sorry.

JUDY. If you're going, go!

NIXON. Judy, I hope you find that rainbow.

JUDY. Dick, I've got rainbows coming out my ass.

*(***NIXON*** turns to go but, shamed by* **DEATH***, returns the ten dollars to the* **AUDIENCE MEMBER***, offers his famous "V" for Victory salute and leaves.)*

JOAN. Judy! I had a fabulous time.

JUDY. Sure, Joanie. We'll do it again sometime.

JOAN. *(with genuine sincerity)* No, really. I was so happy to be invited. "The Best of Everything." Except the part. I wasn't even the lead. Hope Lange. But it's the last time I was in a real Hollywood movie. It was the last time I really felt like a star.

(a wry laugh, then gently)

Oh, darling. Hollywood, purgatory – what's the difference? Either way you watch your life go by while some asshole keeps you on hold.

*(***JOAN*** goes to the door and turns back grandly.)*

JOAN. Merry Christmas to all and to all a good night.

(JOAN *leaves*. **LIBERACE** *approaches* **JUDY**.)

LIBERACE. I'm sorry there's no time for an encore but Mother and I have our dinner engagement with that young –

JUDY. Oh, yeah, right.

LIBERACE. I just wanted to say...I know people made fun of me. And I cried all the way to the bank. But I still cried. Nobody loved me but the fans – and my mother.

(confronting **DEATH***)*

And I've got your number, sister. You know what you are? You're a five-star bitch.

DEATH. Only if you want to live.

LIBERACE. Save it for Susan Hayward.

(to the audience)

I'll be seeing you.

*(***LIBERACE*** *leaves*.)*

LILLIAN. I fought so hard. When the villains were bigger than life, it was easy to be a great lady. But once the shooting stopped...everything's so much easier when you've got someone to hate. I didn't know what the hell to write about. So I re-wrote my life and became a great lady all over again. It wasn't as much fun. I guess I just wanted to have some fun.

(patting **JUDY***'s arm)*

LILLIAN. *(cont.)* Don't worry, Judy. I went up against the committee. It doesn't matter a damn what they think. What matters, is what you think.

(a beat)

You *really* thought I wrote children's books?

JUDY. "Toys In The Attic."

LILLIAN. Two old maids with a brother fixation.

JUDY. And –

LILLIAN. "The Children's Hour?" Two dykes in a boarding school.

JUDY. Oh.

LILLIAN. *(a sudden, hearty laugh)* Hellman's Mayonnaise!

*(**LILLIAN** continues laughing as she exits.)*

BING. Come on, honey. Let's go home.

JUDY. I can't.

*(**BING** cues **ETHEL** who goes to **JUDY**.)*

ETHEL. You think you had a lousy exit – try and top this: I was dead for three days before they even found me. Where the hell did everybody go? The only way I knew how to get 'em back was to keep on plugging.

(gazing wistfully out into the studio)

It sure was great to hear that applause again.

*(tearfully embracing **JUDY**)*

You son-of-a-bitch.

*(As **ETHEL** exits, **DEATH** offers her his hand and she bats him with her handbag.)*

*(**BING** turns regretfully to **JUDY**.)*

BING. You're sure now?

JUDY. Yes.

*(**BING** looks at **DEATH** and pauses, torn.)*

BING. I'll go on and warm 'em up for you.

*(to **DEATH**)*

I'm putty, sir, pure putty in your hands.

*(**BING** exits, humming a song.)*

*(A low wind begins to ruffle the stage curtains. A distant funeral bolls tolls. As it continues, it grows louder. **DEATH** confronts **JUDY**.)*

DEATH. Come, my child.

JUDY. No.

DEATH. Take my hand and follow.

JUDY. I'm not going back there ever, ever again.

DEATH. But you must. Everyone follows.

JUDY. I'm not everyone. I'm Judy Garland – and I've got a show to do.

DEATH. You will be left with nothing.

JUDY. I don't care. Why can't you just...you can't make me!

DEATH. That is true. But I can try.

(On the final gong **DEATH** *raises his cloak to reveal the ruby slippers.)*

(Music under. **JUDY** *gasps, horrified that Death has stolen the one thing that has always protected her. She circles him, her terror growing as he seductively holds out his hand.* **JUDY** *draws closer, hypnotized, but, at the last moment, breaks away. Angered,* **DEATH** *furiously hurls down his cloak and sweeps toward the door. He turns to reach out to* **JUDY** *one final time and, as he does, the set moves off.* **DEATH** *exits.)*

(A spotlight appears downstage center. **JUDY** *walks into it. The music becomes softer and a lone piano plays.)*

JUDY. This last number is a favorite of mine. I hope it's one of yours, too.

(singing)

HAVE YOURSELF
A MERRY...LITTLE...

*(***JUDY** *falters. The music continues.)*

Stop. Stop...please. I – I can't sing this anymore. It's not that I don't wish you a merry little Christmas, you've been so lovely. But I hope you'll understand... forgive me, because at the moment, I'm fresh out.

(The work lights snap on and she crumples.)

JUDY. Oh, God, why am I so frightened?

*(***JUDY** *weeps. After a moment, the* **SAILOR** *enters.)*

SAILOR. Excuse me, Ma'am.

JUDY. Who's there?

SAILOR. It's me. Seaman Russell. I'm looking for Liberace.

JUDY. Oh, dear...he's gone. He's...they're all gone.

SAILOR. Your friends?

JUDY. *(bitterly)* My friends. When the shit hits the fan they all walk away. Backwards and smiling.

SAILOR. Lee said we were going to dinner after the –

JUDY. Right. Midnight supper with mother.

SAILOR. I think it's past his mother's bedtime, if you know what I mean.

JUDY. Oh. I suppose I do. But I never...well, look at you. You're such a big, strong fellow. I never would have thought you were...

SAILOR. Dead?

JUDY. That, too. Now don't blame me for dragging you into this mess, because I don't even know who you are.

SAILOR. I never got the chance to see any of you when you were alive. I figured this was the next best thing.

JUDY. I don't know why you'd want to watch a bunch of old ghosts shuffle around a Christmas tree. What was I thinking? Nixon! Didn't you hear? They practically threw him out of the White House.

SAILOR. That's true. But he ended up quite a statesman. They say he opened the door to China.

JUDY. *Communist* China?

SAILOR. Yes, ma'am.

JUDY. Well, that should make Lilly happy. Maybe. Lillian Hellman. *That's* entertainment. Can't sing, can't dance, can't even schmooze a goddamn puppet.

SAILOR. You know, they made a movie about her.

JUDY. More lies.

SAILOR. Made a helluva good story.

JUDY. Who'd they get to play her? Spencer Tracy? Thank God I booked Ethel. At least she's a trooper. And there's no bullshit with Merman. Poor thing. Dying all alone. What really killed her was her daughter's suicide. So much for the First Lady of the American Musical Theater.

SAILOR. But that's who she was. She still is.

JUDY. *(annoyed)* Speaking of "ladies," what about your side-kick, Liberace?

SAILOR. What about him?

JUDY. Oh, come on. I know he was a wonderful entertainer and there'll never be anyone like him and all that. But let's face it, his whole life was a fraud.

SAILOR. Offstage. But onstage? He was as queer as they come. And they loved him for it.

JUDY. Exactly. Wait a second. How do you know so much, anyway?

SAILOR. I lived longer.

JUDY. Oh. Right. What's the dirt on Crawford?

SAILOR. They made a movie about her, too.

JUDY. The wire hangers?

SAILOR. Afraid so.

JUDY. I knew it. What a phony bitch! I dare you to tell me anything real about Joan Crawford.

SAILOR. She had broad shoulders.

JUDY. Costumes by Adrian.

SAILOR. She was glamorous.

JUDY. Make-up by Westmore.

SAILOR. She sure could act.

JUDY. Directed by Cukor.

SAILOR. She was a movie star.

JUDY. You got me. I'm on to your game, you know. You want me to say something rotten about Bing so you can turn around and tell me about his wonderful legacy and all that. Save your breath. Bing was the best. Of his time. Because believe me, styles are like seasons. They come and boy do they go.

SAILOR. Like Christmas?

JUDY. *(warily)* You mean, "White Christmas?"

SAILOR. Number one record of all time.

JUDY. Still?

SAILOR. It wouldn't seem like Christmas without Bing.

JUDY. *(sarcastic)* Is it my turn?

SAILOR. What would you like to know?

JUDY. Nothing. I don't want to know anything. There was no big hullabaloo when I died. Maybe a couple of fags on Fire Island got drunk and sang "Over The Rainbow" but that's it.

(The SAILOR smiles.)

JUDY. Sorry. I was just a girl singer. It's not like I discovered penicillin or freed the slaves. Judy Garland never saved anybody's life.

SAILOR. You saved mine.

JUDY. What?

SAILOR. The night of your funeral, the police raided a bar in Greenwich Village.

(JUDY folds her arms akimbo and appraises him coolly.)

JUDY. Yeah? So?

SAILOR. Everyone there was so upset about losing you, they decided they weren't going to lose anything else. They stood up for themselves. They fought back. Finally. God, it changed everything. It gave me the chance to be who I am. So in a way, you did. You saved my –

(JUDY slaps him.)

JUDY. You goddamn liar. I think I know when I've been lied to. And I've been lied to ever since people figured out how to make a buck off of me. Yeah. Lying to get me to take pills or come out of a dressing room, or 'sign here, Judy, and you'll never have another worry for the rest of your life.' Right. I know all about liars. I DON'T BUY IT! I WON'T! Do you think you can make me believe I made any difference? Think again. You can't make me believe anything!

SAILOR. That's true. But I can try.

JUDY. *(startled)* Who *are* you?

SAILOR. Don't you have a show to do?

JUDY. *(a rueful laugh)* My 'big comeback?' "Clang, clang, clang, went the trolley." In Hollywood you're only as good as your last picture. Mine flopped.

SAILOR. This isn't Hollywood.

JUDY. No. It's not. But it's too late.

(starting to cry)

Oh, God, I'm so sorry. I tried. But I screwed everything up and I don't know how to fix it.

SAILOR. Maybe you didn't. Maybe everything was the way it was supposed to be, even though some of it was pretty rough. And if even one second of your life had been easier or safer, you wouldn't have been you.

(Music softly underneath.)

SAILOR. Nothing is wasted.

JUDY. Then why can't I let go?

SAILOR. You can let go, Judy. We've got you.

(JUDY looks at him and then the audience.)

JUDY. Does anyone really remember?

(The SAILOR nods gently.)

JUDY. Who are you?

SAILOR. I'm just a fan.

(He kisses her on the cheek and leaves. JUDY watches him go and then contemplates all she has learned.)

(A far-off musical vamp is heard. A beam of pure white light shines down onto the stage behind JUDY.)

(She turns and walks upstage into the light. She looks up and reaches into the beam and forms the famous "Garland pose.")

ANNOUNCER. *(V.O.)* Ladies and gentlemen, Miss Judy Garland.

(In a split second, the front spot hits her and the upstage beam goes out. JUDY turns back to the AUDIENCE with a smile and sings:)

JUDY.

> SEE SKIES OF BLUE
> WHEN CLOUDS ARE GRAY.
> WAKE UP AND MAKE EVERY MORN'…
>
> *(A smile of realization)*
>
> LIKE CHRISTMAS DAY.
> IN EVERYTHING THAT YOU DO,
> KEEP IT EXCITING AND NEW.
> MAKE IT SHINE.
>
> WHY LIVE YOUR LIFE
> IN BLACK AND WHITE
> WHEN YOU CAN HAVE IT IN TECHNICOLOR BRIGHT?
> IF YOU CAN MAKE SOMEONE SMILE,
> YOU'VE GOT A GIFT WORTH YOUR WHILE.
> MAKE IT SHINE!
>
> YES, MAKE IT GLEAM
> AS YOU PURSUE
> THE BEST OF LIFE.
> THE BEST OF YOU.
> AND SO THAT OTHERS WILL SEE
> HOW BRIGHT A SPIRIT CAN BE,
> TAKE IT AND MAKE IT SHINE!

JUDY.	**CHORUS.**
TO GIVE YOUR ALL	OOOH.
IS NOT SO TOUGH.	OOOH.
SUCCEED, BE HAPPY,	OOOH.
THEN TRUST THAT IT'S ENOUGH.	OOOH.
YOUR FEARS ARE OVER AND DONE,	
YOU'VE EARNED A PLACE IN THE SUN.	
MAKE IT SHINE.	MAKE IT SHINE.
THE RAINBOW'S END	AAAAAH.
IS NEVER FAR.	AAAAAH.
IT'S JUST A GLIMMER AWAY	AAAAAH.
FROM WHERE YOU ARE.	AAAAAH.
WHATEVER DREAM THAT YOU HOLD	

HAS GOT TO GLITTER LIKE GOLD…
MAKE IT SHINE.   MAKE IT SHINE.

WHAT'S PAST IS PAST,
AND THAT'S OKAY.
BUT NOW IS NOW.
LIVE FOR TODAY!   LIVE FOR TODAY!

YOUR JOY WILL BEAM LIKE THE DAWN   AAAH.
FROM HERE TO HEAVEN AND ON…   AAAH.
IF YOU JUST MAKE IT SHINE!

(JUDY starts to leave, then hesitates. BING appears in spectral white. JUDY looks on, astounded.)

BING.

THOSE GRAND OLD TIMES
WE KNEW BACK WHEN,
IF WELL-REMEMBERED,
ARE SURE TO COME AGAIN.
A MEMORY SWEET AND SUBLIME
WILL NEVER PERISH WITH TIME.
MAKE IT SHINE.

(One by one, the other characters return dressed in fantastic white costumes. JUDY watches, delighted and deeply moved by each heavenly apparition.)

LILLIAN.

DECRY ALL WRONGS.
DEFY ALL FOES.
TRAVAIL, ASSAIL
AND PREVAIL WITH SIMPLE PROSE.
YOUR LIFE'S A BOOK, DO IT PROUD.
DRAMATIC LICENSE ALLOWED.
MAKE IT SHINE.

JOAN.

BECOME A STAR.
IGNITE THE SCREEN.
BE STRICT.
BE GRAND.
AND YES, BE CLEAN!

(**JOAN** *reveals her hands, covered in rubber gloves and clutching a can of cleanser.*)

JOAN.

WHERE THERE'S A SCRUBBER AND SOAP,
THERE IS A FLICKER OF HOPE.
USE GLOVES!
AND MAKE IT SHINE.

NIXON.

DISLIKED IS FINE,
BUT NOT DISGRACED.
TO ERR IS HUMAN...
MISTAKES CAN BE ERASED.
A LITTLE POLISH IS BOUND
TO TURN YOUR IMAGE AROUND.
MAKE IT SHINE.

ETHEL.

THE WORLD'S A STAGE.
IT'S ALL WE'VE GOT.
AND THERE'S NO BUSINESS I KNOW
LIKE YOU-KNOW-WHAT!
SO WHEN YOU BELT OUT A SONG,
MAKE IT LOUD.
MAKE IT LONNNGGG!
MAKE IT SHINE!

(**LIBERACE** *enters wearing an electric suit that lights up in stages.*)

LIBERACE.

IT MAY TAKE GUTS.
A CERTAIN FLAIR.
A TWINKLE HERE.
A SPARKLE THERE.
BUT WHEN YOU HEAR THAT APPLAUSE,
YOU KNOW THEY LOVE YOU BECAUSE
YOU REALLY MAKE IT SHINE!

(*Music decrescendos. A reprise of "Angel Star" cues Judy's epiphany that she doesn't have to "come back" any longer. All she has to do is move on.*)

ALL (BUT JUDY).

> AAAH!
> AAAH!
> MAKE IT SHINE!
>
> (**JUDY** *summons her courage and, as the music swells, exits upstage to her judgment.*)
>
> WHO KNOWS WHAT WAITS
> AROUND THE BEND?
> WHO CARES?
> JUST WHISTLE YOUR WAY
> TO JOURNEY'S END.
> THE TRIP IS OVER TOO FAST,
> SO MAKE IT GOOD.
> MAKE IT LAST.

LIBERACE.

> MAKE IT SHINE!

JOAN.

> MAKE IT SHINE!

BING.

> MAKE IT SHINE!

LILLIAN.

> MAKE IT SHINE!

NIXON.

> MAKE IT SHINE!

ETHEL.

> MAKE IT SHINE!

ALL.

> MAKE IT SHINE!!
>
> *(They dance joyously,* **BING** *with* **JOAN,** **NIXON** *with* **ETHEL,** **LIBERACE** *with* **LILLIAN.**)

BING. What say we improvise a little cheek to cheek?

ETHEL. C'mon, Veep, let's cut a rug.

NIXON. Uh, Miss Merman, I think you're leading.

ETHEL. You're not so bad yourself.

LIBERACE. Heaven, I'm in heaven!

JOAN. Oh, how I wish I'd made more musicals.

BING. No regrets, Sister Joan, no regrets.

LIBERACE. I feel like we're dancing on air.

LILLIAN. I think we are!

(Offstage the "clang-clang" of a trolley bell is heard. Everyone turns to see the arrival of the oft-mentioned, old-time trolley, decorated in style for style for the holidays.)

ALL.

CLANG, CLANG, CLANG WENT THE TROLLEY!

*(**JUDY**, in white tie and tails, rides up front alongside the motorman, **DEATH**, who wears a jaunty Santa cap.)*

*(The streetcar stops centerstage and **JUDY** jubilantly disembarks to embrace her friends who board the trolley like excited children.)*

JUDY. Hurry, everyone, all aboard!

JOAN. Judy, you look beautiful!

ETHEL. That's one helluva trolley!

LIBERACE. Dibs on the window seat!

LILLIAN. I'm so excited...to be excited!

NIXON. I can't wait for you to meet Mother!

BING. C'mon, gang, let's take it home!

*(**DEATH** clangs the bell, the Christmas lights sparkle and the fantastic vehicle begins to move. They sing one final, triumphant chorus:)*

ALL.

JUST LEAVE BEHIND
ALL CARES YOU KNEW,
AND LOOK AHEAD.
YOU'LL LIKE THE VIEW.

JUDY.

GET READY,
GLORY IS NEAR!

ALL (BUT JUDY).

SO LET 'EM KNOW THAT YOU'RE HERE.

JUDY.

    YOU – MAKE – IT –

ALL.

    SHINE!

    SHINE!!

    SHINE!!!

    (**JUDY** *waves a grateful goodbye to the audience and then, just before the trolley disappears, a star sparkles brightly as they proceed heavenward.*)

    (blackout)

COSTUME PLOT

CHORUS BOYS (2 men, 2 women) – All dressed as male Dickensian Carolers. White puffy-sleeve shirts, red plaid vests, dark pants, and black shoes. Top hats and scarves complete the outfit. They do not have to be dressed exactly alike.

JUDY GARLAND #1 – Red velvet Christmas Dress with white fur trim – Bob Mackie does Dickens. Cowl collar, three quarter length sleeves, floor length full skirt, fur trimmed. Black dance shoes. (See JUDY GARLAND CHRISTMAS SHOW dress.)

JUDY GARLAND #2 – White beaded top with cowl collar, three quarter length sleeves. Dark stretch slacks or Capri pants. Dance slippers. Chic, cool, casual. (See THE JUDY GARLAND SHOW runway segments.) Also: Sheer Cocktail Apron with two pockets (one for hostess tips booklet, one for kazoo).

BING CROSBY – Hunting jacket, dark plaid wool slacks or corduroys, checkered brimmed hat with feather. (Check out Bing's 1950s movies.)

JUDY and **BING** – matching Holiday Aprons.

LIBERACE – Purple velvet dinner jacket, with beaded piano-key lapels. Knitted white glitter scarf with jingle bells. Black tux pants and black shoes. (Remember, this is before his outfits went really wild.)

SAILOR – Dress whites, White sailor cap. Black regulation shoes.

ETHEL MERMAN – Flowered print dress, floppy straw hat, rattan handbag (big enough to hide a record album), chunky jewelry, (see her outfit in movie IT'S A MAD, MAD, MAD, MAD WORLD) and a Hawaiian Lei.

HULA BOYS (2 men) – Skimpy Hawaiian loin cloths in Hawaiian floral patterns: one red/pink, one blue/green.

HULA GIRLS (2 women) – Hawaiian leis, print bikinis and grass skirts.

RICHARD NIXON – Black suit. Black shoes. White shirt. Dark conservative tie. Magic act: Magician's Cape, Trick Top Hat, Purple Swami Turban with Purple Jewel (fits concealed under Top Hat).

CHORUS BOYS (LIFE OF THE PARTY) – Holiday Sweaters and dark slacks, loafers. (1959 Christmas party chorus boys.)

LILLIAN HELLMAN – A conservative, severe gray wool suit with pearls. Skirt is knee length. Gray low heels.

JUDY GARLAND #3 – Little Black Dress. Black sequined jacket with three quarter sleeves and Mandarin collar. Black heels. (See I COULD GO ON SINGING concert outfit.)

DEATH – Black velour cowl and cape. ("The Ghost of Christmas Yet To Come" from A CHRISTMAS CAROL) Act 2 climax: Ruby Slippers and black/white striped socks (like the Witch of the East). Finale: Santa Hat.

JOAN CRAWFORD – Floor-length gown, flowing, glittery and/or light-colored, think Academy Awards, 1952 with shoulder pads (too grand for a guest shot on TV.)

"MAKE IT SHINE" – **BING, LILLIAN, JOAN, NIXON, ETHEL**, and **LIBERACE** appear in white and silver versions of their previous costumes The attempt is to make this look as much like a lavish MGM musical number as possible. The costumes may also slightly caricature these celebrities and "comment on" their foibles. (**BING** could have certain elements of a leprechaun, **JOAN** has white rubber gloves and canister of Dutch Cleanser, **LIBERACE**'s jacket lights up, etc.) Ensemble all in men's white tailcoats, white tuxedo pants, white shoes.

JUDY GARLAND #4 – **JUDY** wears white tie and white tails (see A STAR IS BORN "Gotta Have Me Go With You" outfit, but in white.)

PROPS

Hand mirror
Makeup compact
Wine glass
Golf putter
Jewelry box with recipe
Gold invitations (6)
Hotplate
Copper "grog" pot
Wooden spoon
Grog ingredients
Whiskey flask
Liquor bottles (assorted)
6 "grog" mugs (matching)
Gift box of sticky buns
Napkins
Liberace's candelabra
Hawaiian leis (10)
Ethel's record album
2 ukeleles
Bar glasses (matching set)
Ice bucket, ice, tongs
Hot chocolate mug (Nixon's)
Photo wallet (Ethel's)
Hor dourve tray
Crabcakes
4 gift wrapped boxes
Tinsel
"tips for the hostess" booklet
Old saxophone
"Gone With the Wind" clue on scrap of paper
Kazoo
"Punch" – dragon puppet with detachable mailman hat
Envelopes (kids' letters to Santa)
Letters to Santa (3) to be read
Cigarettes (Lillian's)
2 pocket lighters
2 ashtrays
Sheet music (2 different covers)
Scythe (Death's)
12 oz. Pepsi bottle w straw
Fireplace tools

OTHER TITLES AVAILABLE FROM SAMUEL FRENCH

SCROOGE!

Leslie Bricusse

Holiday Musical / Various m and f / Various Sets

In 1970, renowned writer-composer-lyricist Leslie Bricusse adapted the classic Charles Dickens tale, *A Christmas Carol*, into the hit screen musical *Scrooge!*

Available as a charming stage musical, *Scrooge!* has enjoyed a hugely successful tour of England and a season at London's Dominion Theatre starring the late Anthony Newly. Included are six new songs not performed in the film. Now this sure-fire audience pleaser is available in two versions: as a full-length musical and in a 55-minute adaptation that is ideal for small theatre groups and schools, where it can be performed as a short play or as part of a seasonal concert. Selected pieces from the most popular musical numbers are included in the shortened adaptation.

"If you liked *Phantom of the Opera*, just wait until you see *Scrooge!*"
– Radio 3, Australia

"Wonderful theatre"
– *Yorkshire Evening Post*

"Sensational...it was terrific."
– BBC Radio 2

"Here is a musical on a grand scale - a rollicking frolicking feast of entertainment."
– *The Country Border News*

"Don't miss it!"
– *Swindon Evening Advertiser*